Granny's Ghost and the Deadly Dinner Party

Ghostly Gumshoe Cozy Mysteries Series, Volume 4

Sloane Finley

Published by Ginger and Spice Publishing, 2025.

This is a work of fiction. Similarities to real people, places, or events are entirely coincidental.

GRANNY'S GHOST AND THE DEADLY DINNER PARTY

First edition. July 11, 2025.

ISBN: 979-8231957750

Written by Sloane Finley.

Table of Contents

Chapter 1

I'm standing in the center of my living room, surveying the transformation that's slowly taking place. The usually cozy space has been rearranged to accommodate tonight's charity dinner for the senior center, and my heart is racing with a mixture of excitement and anxiety as I take in the scene.

The antique dining table I inherited from Granny Ingrid dominates the room, expanded to its full glory. White linen tablecloths drape elegantly over the dark wood, and fresh flowers from my garden add splashes of color throughout the room. Crystal glasses catch the light, throwing tiny rainbows across the crisp napkins.

"Everything has to be perfect," I mutter to myself, straightening a fork that's barely out of alignment with its neighbors. The weight of hosting such an important event settles heavily on my shoulders. This dinner isn't just about impressing the town's elite—and all of my grandmother's old friends—it's about securing vital funding for the senior center.

The doorbell chimes, and my heart leaps into my throat, thinking the guests have arrived early, but then I hear a familiar voice calling out.

"Lena! It's me! I've got reinforcements!"

Relief washes over me as I hurry to open the door. Charlie stands there, her arms laden with bags, a wide grin on her face. Her curls are slightly windblown, and her eyes are sparkling with excitement.

"Charlie, you're a lifesaver," I say, ushering her in. "I was starting to panic a little."

She bustles past me into the house, her energy filling the space. "Panic? You? Never! But just in case, I come bearing extra napkins, candles, and a bottle of wine for the chef," she announces, making her way to the kitchen.

As we work, arranging votives and tying ribbon around napkins, Charlie keeps up a steady stream of chatter about town gossip and her latest dating disasters. It's comforting, this easy back-and-forth we've had since childhood.

"Oh, and you'll never guess what happened at the bakery yesterday," Charlie says, her eyes twinkling with mischief. "Old Mrs. Hendricks came in, you know how particular she is about her lemon tarts..."

I listen, nodding and laughing at all the right moments, but part of my mind is still running through my mental checklist for the evening. Charlie must notice my distraction because she suddenly stops mid-story.

"Lena," she says, her tone gentle but firm. "Everything is going to be fine. More than fine, actually. It's going to be amazing, because you've put your heart and soul into this dinner."

As if in response to Charlie's encouragement, a cool breeze whispers through the room, despite all the windows being closed. I smile, knowing it's Granny Ingrid's way of letting me know she's here.

I turn to see Granny Ingrid's spectral form perched on her favorite armchair. Her ghostly figure is translucent but distinct, dressed in her favorite floral dress and pearls, just as I remember her from life.

"Well, well," Granny Ingrid's voice drifts through the room, audible only to me. "This old house hasn't seen a fancy dinner party like this in years. It's about time these walls echoed with laughter again."

I smile, warmth spreading through me at her words. "I hope it lives up to your standards, Granny," I say softly, mindful of Charlie bustling nearby.

Her ghostly eyes twinkle with mischief. "Oh, I'd say it does. Though in my day, we would have polished the silver a bit more thoroughly."

I can't help but roll my eyes. "Granny, please. I've been at this for hours. Besides, most people don't scrutinize the cutlery like you do."

She chuckles, the sound like a whisper of wind chimes. "Oh, I know. I'm just teasing. You've done a marvelous job, Lena. This reminds me of the soirées your grandfather and I used to throw."

As Granny Ingrid regales me with tales of parties past, I can almost see the ghosts of those long-ago gatherings superimposed over my own preparations. The phantom sounds of clinking glasses and peals of laughter seem to echo faintly in the background.

The doorbell chimes again, interrupting Granny Ingrid's story. This time, my heart does a little flip. I smooth down my dress and take a deep breath before opening the door.

Sheriff Mark stands on my porch, looking handsome in a casual blazer and jeans. His warm eyes crinkle at the corners as he smiles at me, and I feel a flutter in my stomach that has nothing to do with pre-dinner nerves.

"Evening, Lena," he says, his deep voice sending a pleasant shiver down my spine. "Looks like I'm right on time to help with any heavy lifting."

I feel a blush creeping up my cheeks. "Hi, Mark. Come on in. I think we've got most things under control, but an extra pair of hands never hurts."

As he steps inside, I'm acutely aware of his presence—the subtle scent of his cologne, the way he fills the space with his tall frame. It's strange seeing him here as my date rather than in his official capacity as sheriff.

"Place looks great," he says, glancing around appreciatively. "You've really transformed it."

"Thanks," I reply, leading him to the living room. "I just hope it's enough to impress the donors. The senior center really needs this fundraiser to be a success."

Mark's expression softens. "I'm sure it will be. You've put so much work into this, Lena. Everyone can see how much you care."

From the corner of my eye, I see Granny Ingrid nodding approvingly. She seems to have a soft spot for Mark, often hinting that he'd make a fine husband. I push that thought aside, focusing on the task at hand.

"Well, since you're offering to help," I say, handing Mark a stack of name cards, "would you mind setting these out? I've marked where each guest should sit."

As Mark begins arranging the cards, Charlie emerges from the kitchen, wiping her hands on a towel. Her eyebrows raise slightly at the sight of the sheriff, and she shoots me a knowing grin.

"Everything's ready in the kitchen, Lena," she reports. "I've got the hors d'oeuvres warming and the wine is chilling. We're all set."

I nod, but as I look around the room, a sudden wave of unease washes over me. Everything looks perfect—too perfect, almost. In my experience, when things seem this ideal, it usually means something is about to go terribly wrong.

"Lena?" Charlie's voice breaks through my thoughts. "You okay? You look like you've seen a ghost." She pauses, glancing around and lowering her voice so Mark can't overhear. "I mean, you know, besides the usual one."

I force a smile. "I'm fine. Just a bit nervous, I guess."

"Don't be," Mark says, coming to stand beside me. His hand brushes mine, a gesture of reassurance. "You've done an amazing job. The guests will love it."

I take a deep breath, trying to shake off the foreboding feeling. "You're right. Both of you. I'm just being silly."

As I move to adjust a vase of flowers, I hear Granny Ingrid's voice, so soft I'm sure only I can hear it. "Trust your instincts, dear. They've never led you astray before."

I pause, my hand on the vase. Granny's right, of course. My instincts have helped me solve more than one mystery in this town. But surely not tonight. Not at a simple charity dinner.

Chapter 2

The doorbell chimes, and I take a deep breath, smooth my dress one last time, and plaster on my most welcoming smile. Showtime.

I open the door to find June Fischer standing on the porch, her silver hair coiffed to perfection and her piercing blue eyes already scanning the entryway behind me. "Lena, darling," she purrs, air-kissing my cheeks. "How lovely of you to host this little soirée."

"Welcome, Mrs. Fischer," I reply, stepping aside to let her in. "I'm so glad you could make it. May I take your coat?"

June shrugs off her fur stole, handing it to me with a dismissive wave. "I do hope you've stored the good wine somewhere cool, dear. I can't tell you how much I detest room-temperature Chardonnay."

"Of course, Mrs. Fischer. We have a lovely selection chilling as we speak," I assure her, hanging up her coat.

June sweeps into the living room, her designer dress rustling as she moves. Her gaze immediately locks onto the seating chart near the dining table. "Oh, how quaint," she says, her voice dripping with false sweetness. "You've taken the time to arrange our seating. So very... thoughtful."

I watch as her eyes narrow, scanning the names. Her perfectly manicured nail taps against the chart. "I see you've invited that boorish Pete Granger," she says, her lip curling slightly. "I do hope he remembers which fork to use this time. And Gordy Jacobs? Really, Lena, I thought this was supposed to be a respectable gathering."

I force a smile, trying to keep my tone light. "We're hoping to bring together all of the senior center's most generous supporters, Mrs. Fischer. I'm sure everyone will be on their best behavior."

June lets out a delicate snort. "Well, we shall see about that, won't we?" She turns to me, patting my arm condescendingly. "Do be a dear and point me toward the wine. I have a feeling I'll need it to get through this evening."

As I direct June to the bar, where Charlie is pouring drinks, I overhear her mutter under her breath, "Gordy Jacobs and Harold Dawson in the same room. This should be interesting."

Before I can ponder her words, the doorbell rings again. This time, it's Harold Dawson standing on the threshold, his usually impeccable appearance slightly disheveled. His tie is askew, and there's a tightness around his eyes that I've never seen before.

"Good evening, Mr. Dawson," I greet him, immediately picking up on his tension. "Is everything okay?"

Harold starts slightly, as if pulled from deep thought. "Ah, Lena. Yes, yes, everything's fine. Just a bit preoccupied with work matters, I'm afraid. Nothing to worry about." He attempts a smile, but it doesn't do much to ease the tension.

As I lead Harold into the living room, I can't shake the feeling that there's more to his distraction than mere work stress. He moves stiffly, his eyes darting around the room as if he's searching for someone—or maybe avoiding someone.

"Can I get you a drink, Mr. Dawson?" I offer, trying to put him at ease.

"Yes, please. Scotch, if you have it. Neat." His voice is strained, and he tugs at his collar nervously.

As I pour his drink, June saunters over, her smile shark-like. "Harold, darling. How lovely to see you. How's that new development of yours coming along? I heard there were some... issues with the zoning permits."

Harold's grip tightens on his glass. "Everything's proceeding as planned, June. Thank you for your concern."

"Oh, I'm sure it is," June replies, her tone suggesting otherwise. "It would be such a shame if anything were to derail the project. Especially given your recent investments."

Before Harold can respond, the doorbell chimes again. Grateful for the interruption, I excuse myself to answer it.

The next arrival is Clara Benton, head of the senior center and ostensibly the guest of honor for the evening. Her smile is bright as she greets me, but I notice her gaze keeps drifting over my shoulder, as if she's expecting someone else to appear at any moment.

"Lena, dear, this is wonderful," Clara gushes, squeezing my hand. "The senior center is so grateful for your support. I just know tonight will be a smashing success."

As I lead Clara into the living room, she continues, "I can't tell you how much this means to us. With the recent... well, let's just say this fundraiser couldn't have come at a better time."

I raise an eyebrow at her cryptic comment. "Is everything okay at the center, Clara? You know you can always come to me if there are any problems."

Clara's smile falters for a moment before she regains her composure. "Oh, it's nothing we can't handle. Just the usual budget constraints, you know how it is. I don't want to monopolize too much of your time this evening, though. Just point me toward the wine and I'll be on my way."

As Clara mingles with the other guests, I observe her carefully. Despite her cheery demeanor, there's an undercurrent of nervousness in her movements. She laughs a little too loudly at June's barbed jokes, and her hand trembles slightly as she accepts a glass of wine from Charlie.

The atmosphere in the room shifts noticeably when Pete Granger arrives. His burly frame fills the doorway, and his craggy face is set in its usual scowl. "Evening," he grunts, nodding curtly as he steps inside.

"Welcome, Mr. Granger," I say, trying to inject some warmth into the suddenly chilly atmosphere. "Can I take your jacket?"

Pete shrugs off his worn leather jacket, revealing a slightly rumpled shirt underneath. "Thanks," he mutters. "Where's the booze?"

I point him toward the bar, watching as he makes his way into the living room, his eyes scanning the gathered guests. When his gaze lands on Harold Dawson, the temperature in the room seems to drop by several degrees.

"Dawson," Pete says, his voice gruff.

Harold straightens, his posture stiffening. "Granger," he replies, his tone clipped.

The two men stare at each other for a long moment, the tension between them almost palpable. I glance at Charlie, who raises an eyebrow in silent communication. Clearly, there's some history here that we're not privy to.

I'm beginning to wonder if an open bar was the best idea for this dinner party. Then again, I think some of the attendees would already be in open rebellion without it.

June, never one to miss an opportunity for drama, sidles up to the two men. "Well, isn't this cozy? Pete, darling, I didn't know you owned anything other than that dreadful uniform. And look, you've even managed to button your shirt correctly. Bravo."

Pete's scowl deepens. "Can it, June. I'm not here for your amusement."

"No?" June feigns surprise. "Then why are you here? Surely not for the stimulating conversation."

Before Pete can retort, the front door swings open dramatically, and in strides Gordy Jacobs, the last of our guests to arrive. His silver hair is slicked back, and his expensive suit practically gleams in the light of the chandelier.

"Ladies and gentlemen," Gordy announces, his arms spread wide, "the party can now officially begin!"

A ripple of forced laughter moves through the room. Gordy moves among the guests like a shark through water, his charm barely concealing a predatory edge.

"June, my dear," he says, approaching Mrs. Fischer. "Still wearing that old necklace, I see. Pity you never let me replace it with something more substantial." His words are honey-coated barbs, and I see June's knuckles whiten around her glass.

June's smile is brittle as she responds, "Oh, Gordy. Still trying to buy affection, I see. How... predictable."

Gordy chuckles, seemingly unfazed by her barb. He then turns to Pete, his smile sharpening. "Pete, old boy. Still playing at being a cop? I thought you'd have found a real job by now."

Pete's scowl deepens, but he says nothing, merely taking a long swig of his drink.

"And Harold!" Gordy exclaims, clapping the visibly uncomfortable man on the shoulder. "How's that new development coming along? I heard there might be some environmental concerns. Such a shame if anything were to delay the project."

Harold's face pales slightly. "Everything's under control, Gordy. No need for concern."

As the guests settle into uneasy conversation, I can't help but notice the undercurrents of tension rippling through the room. June's eyes keep darting between Gordy and Harold, her expression a mix of disdain and something deeper—regret, perhaps? Clara seems to be avoiding direct conversation with both Pete and Gordy, focusing her attention on the other guests with an almost manic intensity.

I feel a cool breeze brush past me and hear Granny Ingrid's whisper in my ear. "Keep your eyes open, Lena. There's more going on here than meets the eye."

I nod imperceptibly, agreeing with my ghostly grandmother. The carefully laid plans for a smooth, successful fundraising dinner seem to be unraveling before my eyes. As I move to call everyone to the table, I can't shake the feeling that this evening is balanced on a knife's edge, ready to tip into chaos at any moment.

"Ladies and gentlemen," I announce, trying to inject some warmth into the chilly atmosphere, "dinner will be served shortly. Shall we move to the dining room?"

As the guests begin to file towards the dining table, I catch snippets of hushed conversations:

"We need to talk, Gordy. This can't wait," Clara mutters urgently.

"Not now," Gordy hisses back. "After dinner. Don't make a scene."

Meanwhile, Pete corners Harold near the doorway. "You better watch your step, Dawson. I'm onto you."

Harold's reply is too low for me to hear, but the tension in his shoulders speaks volumes.

I exchange a worried glance with Charlie as we guide everyone to their seats. Whatever is brewing beneath the surface of this gathering, I have a sinking feeling that it's about to boil over. And as the hostess, I'm right in the middle of it all.

Chapter 3

As I guide the last of my guests to their seats, I feel a warm hand on my lower back. I turn to find Mark standing close, his eyes filled with concern.

"You're doing great, Lena," he murmurs, his voice low enough for only me to hear. "But I've got to say, I've never seen such a tense group at a charity dinner before. Is it always like this at the senior center?"

I shake my head, keeping my voice equally low. "No, this is... unusual. I knew there were some old rivalries, but I never realized how deep they ran."

Mark nods, his brow furrowing. "I'm picking up on a lot of undercurrents here. Seems like there are more long-running feuds and rivalries simmering just under the surface than I ever realized. And I'm the sheriff, for crying out loud."

"Tell me about it," I sigh. "I'm starting to wonder if putting all these people in one room was a mistake."

"Hey," Mark says, giving me a reassuring smile. "You're doing an amazing job. Just keep being your charming self, and I'm sure everything will work out fine."

As Mark moves to take his seat, I feel a familiar chill in the air. Granny Ingrid's ghostly form materializes beside me, her expression thoughtful.

"Well, well," she murmurs, her voice audible only to me. "What a gathering of old grudges and buried secrets we have here. Lena, dear, you might want to keep a close eye on our friend Gordy. He's at the center of more drama than you might realize."

I raise an eyebrow, pretending to adjust a place setting as I whisper, "What do you mean, Granny?"

Ingrid's spectral form glides around the table, pausing behind Gordy's chair. "Oh, Gordy was quite the ladies' man back in the day. Still is, from what I can see. His relationships with women like June and Clara were far from innocent, I can tell you that much."

I nearly drop the fork I'm straightening. "June and Clara? But they're so different..."

"Gordy never did have a type," Ingrid chuckles. "He liked variety. But it's not just the ladies you need to watch out for. See how Pete keeps glaring at him?"

I glance over to where Pete is sullenly nursing his drink, indeed shooting daggers at Gordy with his eyes.

"Pete and Gordy have never seen eye to eye," Ingrid continues. "There were some... incidents in the past. Nothing ever proven, of course, but Pete's always believed Gordy was up to no good."

As I circulate the room, topping up wine glasses and making sure everyone is comfortable, I keep an ear out for any interesting snippets of conversation. Ingrid floats alongside me, offering commentary.

"Oh, Harold and June used to be quite the item," she whispers as we pass the pair, who are studiously avoiding each other's gaze. "Until Gordy came along, that is. June dropped Harold like a hot potato, but it didn't last with Gordy either. Left both men bitter, if you ask me."

I nod imperceptibly, filing away this information. As I approach Clara to refill her glass, I overhear a heated exchange between her and Harold.

"...can't keep covering for you, Clara," Harold hisses, his face flushed. "The money has to come from somewhere."

Clara's response is cut short as she notices my approach, her face immediately morphing into a bright smile. "Lena, darling! This wine is simply divine. You must tell me where you got it."

I play along, discussing the wine's origins while my mind races. What money were they talking about? And why would Harold be covering for Clara?

As I make my way back to the kitchen to check on the main course, Ingrid's ghost falls into step beside me.

"Lena, dear," she says, her voice uncharacteristically serious. "I can't put my finger on it, but something feels off about tonight. More than just their usual squabbles. Be on your guard."

I nod, a sense of unease settling in my stomach. "I feel it too, Granny. But what can I do?"

"Keep your eyes and ears open," Ingrid advises. "And trust your instincts. You've got good ones, just like your old Granny."

With a wink, Ingrid's form fades away, leaving me alone in the kitchen. I take a deep breath, centering myself before picking up the first course to serve.

As I re-enter the dining room, the tension is palpable. Gordy is holding court at one end of the table, his voice carrying over the muted conversations.

"...and that's when I told the governor, 'You can't make an omelet without breaking a few eggs!' He loved that, didn't he, Clara?"

Clara forces a laugh, her eyes darting nervously to Pete, who's scowling into his salad.

"Yes, well," Clara says, her voice strained, "I'm sure the governor appreciates your... unique perspective, Gordy."

"Oh, he does more than appreciate it," Gordy boasts, winking at June. "He values my opinion very highly. In fact, just the other day, he called me about a certain piece of legislation..."

"Oh, spare us your name-dropping, Gordy," June interrupts, her voice sharp. "We're all aware of your supposed connections."

The way she says "connections" makes it sound like a dirty word. Gordy's eyes narrow slightly, but his smile remains fixed in place.

"Now, now, June," he chides. "No need to be jealous. Just because some of us have managed to maintain our influence over the years..."

Pete snorts derisively, drawing everyone's attention. "Influence? Is that what we're calling it these days?"

The room falls silent, the tension ratcheting up another notch. I quickly step in, hoping to defuse the situation.

"Who's ready for the main course?" I ask brightly, gesturing to Charlie, who's entering with a large serving platter.

As we serve the food, I catch Mark's eye. He gives me a subtle nod, indicating he's ready to step in if things get out of hand. I appreciate his support, but I hope it won't come to that.

Once everyone is served, I take my seat, hoping the act of eating will keep any further arguments at bay. For a few minutes, the only sounds are the clink of cutlery and murmured compliments about the food.

But the peace doesn't last long. Harold clears his throat, addressing Gordy. "So, Gordy, I hear there's been some interest in that old warehouse property of yours. Any plans to sell?"

Gordy's eyes glitter with something that looks like triumph. "As a matter of fact, Harold, I've had a very interesting offer. But

I'm not at liberty to discuss the details just yet. You understand, I'm sure."

Harold's knuckles whiten around his fork. "Of course. I just hope you'll consider the impact on the community before making any hasty decisions."

"Oh, I always consider the community," Gordy replies smoothly. "It's why I'm here tonight, after all. Supporting our dear Clara's efforts at the senior center."

Clara flinches slightly at the mention of her name, and I notice Pete watching her reaction closely.

"Speaking of the senior center," Pete interjects, his voice gruff, "I've been meaning to ask about those safety upgrades we discussed, Clara. Any progress on that front?"

Clara's smile is strained as she responds, "We're... working on it, Pete. These things take time, you know. And money."

"Money that seems to be in short supply lately," Pete growls, his gaze flicking between Clara and Gordy.

The tension in the room ratchets up another notch. I feel a cool breeze brush past me and hear Granny Ingrid's whisper in my ear.

"Careful, Lena. Things are coming to a head faster than I expected."

I nod imperceptibly, my mind racing. What could I do to steer the conversation to safer ground?

Before I can think of anything, June speaks up, her voice dripping with false sweetness. "Oh, Clara, I've been meaning to ask. How is dear Robert these days? I haven't seen him around town lately."

Clara's face pales visibly. "He's fine. Traveling for work."

"Is he now?" June presses, a predatory gleam in her eye. "How interesting. I could have sworn I saw him just the other day, having a rather intense conversation with our friend Gordy here."

All eyes turn to Gordy, who for once seems caught off guard. He recovers quickly, though, his trademark smirk sliding back into place.

"Now, June," he chides, "you know I have conversations with lots of people. It's part of being a pillar of the community."

Pete snorts again, louder this time. "Pillar of the community? That's rich, coming from you, Gordy."

"And what's that supposed to mean?" Gordy demands, his jovial mask slipping for a moment.

"I think you know exactly what it means," Pete growls, half-rising from his chair.

I exchange a panicked glance with Mark, who's already starting to stand. But before either of us can intervene, there's a loud crash from the kitchen, followed by Charlie's startled yelp.

"Lena!" she calls, her voice strained. "Could you come here for a second? We've got a bit of a situation!"

Grateful for the interruption, I quickly excuse myself and hurry to the kitchen, leaving the simmering tensions behind me. As I push through the swinging door, I find Charlie standing amidst a sea of broken glass, a look of sheepish apology on her face.

"I'm so sorry, Lena," she says, gesturing to the mess. "I was trying to get the dessert ready and I knocked over the tray of glasses. I didn't mean to interrupt, but I didn't know what else to do."

I take in the scene, a wave of relief washing over me. "Oh, Charlie," I sigh, "you have no idea how perfect your timing is. Things out there are about to boil over."

Charlie's eyes widen. "That bad, huh? Want me to fake a kitchen fire? I could probably manage a small grease fire if it would help."

I can't help but laugh, some of the tension easing from my shoulders. "Let's save that for a real emergency. For now, let's just clean this up and get dessert ready. With any luck, sugar will sweeten some of those sour moods out there."

As we work to clean up the broken glass, I fill Charlie in on the tensions brewing in the dining room. Her eyes grow wider with each revelation.

"Geez, Lena," she whispers, "it sounds like you're hosting a powder keg, not a charity dinner. What are you going to do?"

I shake my head, at a loss. "I don't know, Charlie. I don't know."

Just then, I feel the familiar chill that signals Granny Ingrid's presence. She materializes next to us, her expression grave.

"Lena, dear," she says urgently, "you need to get back out there. I've got a bad feeling about this, and you should always trust a dead woman's intuition."

As if on cue, my nose starts to twitch—an annoying tic, but one that almost always means trouble is in the air.

"You feel it, too," Granny says, more of a statement than a question. "You always have had a nose for trouble."

I nod, taking a deep breath to steel myself. "Okay, Granny. I'm going. Charlie, can you handle things in here?"

Charlie gives me a mock salute. "Aye aye, captain. Go save your dinner party. I'll have dessert ready in ten minutes."

With one last grateful smile at Charlie, I square my shoulders and head back to the dining room, Granny Ingrid's spectral form floating beside me.

As I push through the door, the scene that greets me makes my blood run cold. Pete is on his feet, leaning across the table toward Gordy, his face red with anger. Gordy, for his part, looks more amused than intimidated, which seems to be infuriating Pete even more.

"You think you're untouchable, don't you, Jacobs?" Pete is saying, his voice low and dangerous. "But I'm onto you. All of you."

His gaze sweeps the table, lingering on Clara, who looks like she might faint at any moment.

Mark is on his feet too, his hand outstretched in a calming gesture. "Now, Pete," he says, his voice carrying the authority of his office, "let's all just calm down. This isn't the time or place for—"

But before Mark can finish, Gordy lets out a laugh that cuts through the tension like a knife. "Oh, Pete," he chuckles, shaking his head. "Always the crusader. But you know what they say about people who live in glass houses..."

Pete's face goes from red to purple. "Why, you—"

I step forward, my heart pounding. "Dessert!" I announce, my voice unnaturally high. "Who's ready for dessert?"

All eyes turn to me, and for a moment, the tension in the room seems to waver. Then, slowly, Pete sinks back into his chair, his glare never leaving Gordy's face.

"Wonderful idea, Lena," June trills, her voice brittle. "I'm simply dying to taste whatever delightful confection you've prepared."

As if on cue, Charlie pushes through the door, wheeling in a cart laden with individual chocolate soufflés. The rich, sweet scent fills the air, and I see some of the tension leave the room as people turn their attention to the dessert.

But as Charlie begins serving, I can't shake the feeling that this is just the calm before the storm. Granny Ingrid's words echo in my mind: "Something feels off about tonight."

I catch Mark's eye across the table, and he gives me a reassuring nod. Whatever happens next, at least I'm not facing it alone.

Chapter 4

As Charlie finishes serving the soufflés, a hush falls over the room. For a moment, the only sound is the gentle clink of spoons against china as guests savor the decadent dessert. I allow myself a brief sigh of relief, hoping that perhaps the worst of the evening is behind us.

But then Gordy Jacobs pushes back his chair, the scraping sound jarring in the quiet room. He stands, raising his wine glass with a flourish. My heart sinks. I know that look in his eye—he's about to put on a show.

"Ladies and gentlemen," Gordy announces, his voice carrying easily across the table. "I'd like to propose a toast."

All eyes turn to him, some wary, others curious. I catch Mark's gaze across the table, and he gives me a subtle shrug. There isn't much he can do about poorly-timed showmanship or bad manners. Unless someone breaks the law, he's just another guest here, powerless to intervene.

Gordy clears his throat dramatically. "First, I'd like to thank our lovely hostess, Lena, for opening her beautiful home to us this evening. Your grandmother was a long-time supporter and friend, and I know she'd be proud that you're continuing her philanthropic traditions." He raises his glass in my direction, and I force a smile, nodding in acknowledgment.

"And of course," Gordy continues, his smile sharpening, "we mustn't forget the reason we're all here—our dear Clara and her tireless work at the senior center."

Clara shifts uncomfortably in her seat, her smile strained as Gordy turns his attention to her.

"Clara, my dear," he says, his tone dripping with false sincerity, "your dedication to our community's elders is truly admirable. Why, I can't tell you how many times I've heard you say how much the center means to you. Almost as if it were your own personal piggy bank, eh?"

My nose twitches as a few nervous titters ripple through the group. Clara's face flushes red, but she remains silent, her knuckles white around her wine glass.

Gordy's gaze sweeps the table, landing on June. "And let's not forget our other pillars of the community. June, darling, your contributions over the years have been unforgettable. Much like that necklace of yours—a true antique, isn't it?"

June's eyes narrow dangerously. "Not as antique as some people's jokes, Gordy dear," she retorts, her voice syrupy sweet.

Gordy chuckles, seemingly unfazed. "Ah, June. Always quick with a quip. It's part of your charm. Along with your, ah, enduring youthfulness. Tell me, what is your secret? Besides your generous donations to certain medical professionals, of course."

A collective intake of breath follows this barb. I glance at Mark again, silently pleading for help, but he looks as lost as I feel. This is spiraling out of control fast.

"But enough about the past," Gordy continues, his voice rising slightly. "Let's talk about the future. Specifically, the future of our beloved senior center."

He pauses for effect, his gaze sweeping the table once more. "As you all know, I've been a long-time champion of the center and everything it stands for. My financial contributions have been, shall we say, substantial. In fact, I daresay the center wouldn't be standing without my generosity."

Pete snorts derisively, but Gordy presses on, ignoring him.

"And I'm pleased to announce that my support will continue. In fact, I have some exciting news about a new development that will ensure the center's future for years to come."

Clara's head snaps up at this, her eyes wide with a mixture of surprise and what looks like fear. Harold leans forward, his brow furrowed in concern.

"Gordy," Harold interjects, "perhaps this isn't the best time—"

But Gordy waves him off. "Nonsense, Harold. When better to share good news than among friends?" His smile is triumphant as he surveys the table. "Friends who have known each other for so long. Who share so many secrets."

The tension in the room is back in full force. I can almost feel the air crackling with unspoken accusations and barely contained anger.

"To the future," Gordy declares, raising his glass high. "And to the interesting times that lie ahead."

He takes a long sip of his wine, his eyes challenging as he looks at each guest in turn. Reluctantly, the others raise their glasses, murmuring the toast.

As Gordy sits back down, he makes one final remark, his voice low but carrying in the silent room. "Of course, the future isn't set in stone. Things can change in an instant. Fortunes rise and fall. Secrets come to light. It's all part of the game, isn't it?"

The silence that follows is deafening. I clear my throat, desperate to break the tension. "Well, thank you for that interesting toast, Gordy. Shall we enjoy our dessert?"

There's a collective murmur of agreement as people turn their attention to their soufflés. I take a bite of mine, but the rich chocolate tastes like ashes in my mouth. The air feels thick with unspoken threats and simmering resentments.

Suddenly, a strangled gasp breaks the uneasy quiet. All heads turn toward Gordy, who is clutching at his throat, his face turning an alarming shade of red.

For a moment, everyone seems frozen in shock. Then Gordy's chair tips backward as he collapses to the floor, and chaos erupts.

"Oh my God!" Clara shrieks, jumping to her feet. "Gordy!"

Pete is already moving, pushing past the others to kneel beside Gordy's prone form. "Someone call 911!" he barks, his police training kicking in.

Mark is on his feet too, phone already in hand. "I'm on it," he says, his voice steady despite the panic around him.

June stands, her face pale. "Is he... is he having a heart attack?"

"Doesn't look like it," Pete growls, his fingers on Gordy's neck, checking for a pulse. "Looks more like poisoning."

A collective gasp ripples through the room. I feel as if the floor has dropped out from under me. Poisoning? At my dinner party?

"That's impossible," I say, my mind reeling. "How could he be poisoned?"

Harold's voice cuts through the chaos, sharp with accusation. "Well, Lena, you did serve the food. Perhaps you can tell us?"

I stare at him in shock, unable to believe what I'm hearing. "Are you suggesting that I...? That's absurd!"

"Is it?" June chimes in, her earlier animosity toward Gordy seemingly forgotten in light of this new drama. "You did disappear into the kitchen quite a bit during dinner."

“I was checking on the food!” I don’t even try to stop my voice from rising with indignation. “Charlie was with me the whole time. Tell them, Charlie!”

But when I turn to look for Charlie, I realize she’s not in the room. My heart sinks as I remember she stayed in the kitchen to clean up.

Mark steps forward, his voice calm but authoritative. “Let’s not jump to conclusions. The paramedics are on their way. Until then, nobody leaves this room. Understood?”

There’s a murmur of reluctant agreement. I look around at my guests and see suspicion and fear in their eyes. How did a simple charity dinner turn into this nightmare?

As if in answer to my unspoken question, I feel a familiar chill beside me. Granny Ingrid’s ghostly form materializes, her face grave.

“Oh, Lena,” she sighs, her voice audible only to me. “I’m afraid this is only the beginning. The secrets in this room run deeper than you know.”

I swallow hard, watching as Pete continues to perform CPR on Gordy’s unmoving form. The sound of distant sirens reaches us, growing louder by the second.

One thing’s for certain—this is no longer just a dinner party. It’s a crime scene. And somehow, I’ve found myself at the center of it all.

Chapter 5

The room erupts into chaos as Gordy's body lies motionless on the floor. Pete continues CPR, his face red with exertion, while Clara hovers nearby, her hands clasped over her mouth in horror.

"Oh my God, oh my God," she repeats, her voice barely above a whisper. "This can't be happening."

June, on the other hand, has found her voice and is using it to full effect. "Well, I never!" she exclaims, her shrill tone cutting through the panicked murmurs. "In all my years, I've never seen such a thing! Clara, darling, you must be beside yourself. After all, weren't you and Gordy having quite the heated discussion earlier?"

Clara's head snaps up, her eyes wide with shock. "What? No, I... we were just talking about the center. Nothing more!"

"Oh, come now," June presses, her voice dripping with false concern. "We all saw how agitated you were. And now this... it does make one wonder, doesn't it?"

"That's enough, June," I interject, trying to keep my voice steady. "This isn't the time for accusations."

Just then, Charlie bursts through the kitchen door, her eyes widening as she takes in the scene. For a moment, she stands frozen, then something seems to click into place. She straightens her shoulders and claps her hands loudly.

"Alright, everyone," she calls out, her voice carrying over the din. "I need you all to step back and give Sheriff Mark and Officer Pete some room to work. Those of you who aren't directly helping, please move to the living room. Now!"

There's something in Charlie's tone that brooks no argument. Even June, mid-accusation, snaps her mouth shut and begins to shuffle toward the living room.

As Charlie herds the guests away from Gordy's prone form, I catch her eye and mouth a silent 'thank you.' She gives me a quick nod before turning back to the task at hand.

As the guests file into the living room, I overhear snippets of their hushed conversations:

"...never seen anything like it..." "...do you think it was his heart?" "...always knew Gordy would go out with a bang..."

I shake my head, trying to clear it. This isn't happening. This can't be happening.

Suddenly, I notice Harold edging toward the front door, his face ashen. "I... I need to go," he mumbles, reaching for the doorknob. "I can't... I can't be here."

I quickly step in front of him, blocking his path. "I'm sorry, Harold, but no one can leave yet. We need to figure out what happened, and I'm sure Mark will want a word with all the guests."

Harold's eyes dart around wildly, reminding me of a trapped animal. "You don't understand," he hisses, his voice low and urgent. "I have to leave. Now."

Before I can respond, Granny Ingrid's spectral form appears beside me. "Don't let him go, Lena," she warns. "He knows something. I can feel it."

I steel myself, meeting Harold's panicked gaze. "I'm sorry, but you'll have to stay. Sheriff's orders."

As if on cue, Mark's voice carries from the dining room. "Nobody leaves until we've sorted this out. Lena, can you make sure everyone stays put?"

Harold slumps in defeat, shuffling back toward the living room. I follow close behind, my mind racing. What could Harold be so desperate to get away from?

As we enter the living room, June's voice rises above the murmurs once again. "Well, I for one think it's clear what happened here," she announces. "Poor Gordy was poisoned. And I think we all know who had the most to gain from his unfortunate demise."

All eyes turn to Clara, who has sunk into an armchair, her face buried in her hands. She looks up, her eyes red-rimmed and filled with tears. "How can you say that?" she chokes out. "Gordy was my friend. He... he was helping the center. Why would I want to hurt him?"

"Oh, please," June scoffs. "We all know the center's been struggling. And Gordy, bless his soul, was never one to give something for nothing. What did he want in return, Clara? What was the price of his 'generosity'?"

Clara flinches as if she's been slapped. "You don't know what you're talking about," she whispers, but there's a flicker of... something in her eyes. Guilt? Fear?

Pete chooses that moment to enter the room, his face grim. "The paramedics are here," he announces. "They're... they're pronouncing him dead at the scene."

A collective gasp ripples through the room. It's one thing to suspect, another to know for certain. Gordy Jacobs, the larger-than-life figure who has loomed over our town for as long as anyone can remember, is gone.

"Murder," June breathes. "It must be murder."

"We don't know that," Mark interjects, following Pete into the room. He's slipped fully into sheriff mode now, his voice carrying the weight of authority. "Let's not jump to conclusions. The medical examiner will determine cause of death."

"But surely," Harold speaks up, his voice shaky, "surely it's obvious? He collapsed right after drinking the wine. It must have been poisoned."

I feel the weight of several gazes fall on me. After all, I was the one who served the wine.

"Now hold on," Charlie says, stepping forward. "Lena and I prepared everything together. I can vouch for her—there was no opportunity for anyone to tamper with the food or drink in the kitchen."

"Unless you're in on it too," June mutters, but quiets under Charlie's glare.

Mark holds up his hands, calling for silence. "Okay, everyone. I know this is a shock, and we're all upset. But right now, we need to focus on facts. I'm going to need to take statements from each of you about what you saw and heard tonight."

A chorus of protests rises, but Mark silences them with a look. "I know it's late, and I know you're all shaken. But a man is dead, and we need to understand why. So please, cooperate with me on this."

As Mark begins to organize the questioning, I feel a familiar chill beside me. Granny Ingrid's ghostly form shimmers into view, her expression grave.

"Oh, Lena," she sighs. "What a tangled web we find ourselves in. Keep your wits about you, dear. There's more going on here than meets the eye."

I nod imperceptibly, my mind whirling. How did my simple charity dinner turn into a crime scene? And more importantly, what am I going to do about it?

As I watch Mark begin to question June, her voice rising indignantly as she recounts her version of events, I make a decision. I may not be a trained detective, but I feel like I'm a pretty good judge of personality—and there were a lot of strong personalities on display tonight.

With Granny Ingrid by my side and Charlie watching my back, I steel myself for what's to come. It's going to be a long night, but I'm determined to get to the bottom of this mystery.

After all, in a small town like ours, secrets have a way of coming to light whether people want them to or not. And something tells me that by the time this night is over, we're going to uncover more secrets than anyone bargained for.

As I look over the remains of the charity dinner that has turned into a murder investigation, I catch Charlie's eye. She gives me a subtle nod, understanding passing between us without words. We're in this together, come what may.

Chapter 6

As the room buzzes with accusations and fearful whispers, I feel that familiar chill beside me as Granny Ingrid's spectral form shimmers into view.

"Lena, dear," she murmurs, "I need to tell you something important. Earlier, when everyone was arriving, I overheard Clara and Gordy having a heated argument in the hallway. I didn't think much of it at the time, but now it feels like it could be something worth looking into."

My eyes widen, but I manage to keep my face neutral, not wanting to draw attention to the fact that I'm seemingly talking to thin air. "What did you hear, Granny?" I whisper, pretending to adjust a nearby vase.

Ingrid's ghostly form leans in closer. "I couldn't catch everything, but Clara was upset about something Gordy was planning. She kept saying, 'You can't do this, Gordy. It's not right.' And Gordy... well, he just laughed it off in that way of his. Said something about how 'right' doesn't matter when there's money to be made."

I process this information, my mind racing. Could this argument have escalated to murder? It seems impossible, and yet...

"There's more," she continues, her voice low and urgent. "You remember how I told you Gordy used to flirt with June back in the day? Well, it seems he'd started up again recently. I saw them together at the park across the street last week, looking awfully cozy for two people who claim to despise each other."

I raise an eyebrow at this. June and Gordy? That's a complication I hadn't considered. "But Granny," I whisper, "June's been nothing but hostile toward Gordy all night. Why would she—"

"Oh, Lena," Ingrid sighs, a hint of amusement in her otherworldly voice, "you've got a lot to learn about the complexities of romance, especially among us older folks. Sometimes the line between love and hate is thinner than you'd think. And June... well, she's always been the jealous type. If she thought Gordy was playing her..."

I nod slowly, piecing together the information. Gordy had no shortage of enemies, that much was clear. But which one of them would go so far as to poison him? Clara with her mysterious argument? June with her potential jealousy? Or someone else entirely?

Taking a deep breath, I try to calm my racing thoughts. I need to approach this logically, like the amateur sleuth I fancy myself to be. Gordy had made plenty of enemies over the years—that much was obvious from the tension at dinner. Any one of them could potentially be responsible for his death.

There was Clara, of course, with her mysterious financial ties to Gordy and the argument Granny Ingrid had overheard. Then there was June, with her complex history with Gordy and her sharp tongue. Harold, who had seemed so eager to leave earlier—what was he hiding? And Pete, whose long-standing grudge against Gordy was no secret.

Each of them had motive, but which one had the opportunity? And more importantly, which one had actually gone through with it?

I scan the room, taking in the tense faces of my guests. June is still holding court, her voice rising and falling as she recounts her version of events to a stony-faced Mark. Clara sits alone in a corner, her face pale and her hands trembling slightly. Harold paces near the window, his eyes darting nervously around the room. And Pete stands by the door, his arms crossed and his expression unreadable.

Making a decision, I move toward Mark, waiting for a lull in June's monologue. "Mark," I say quietly, touching his arm to get his attention. "Can I speak with you for a moment? In private?"

Mark nods, excusing himself from June, who looks affronted at the interruption. We move to a quiet corner of the room, and I take a deep breath before speaking.

"I... I overheard something earlier," I begin, hating the partial lie but knowing I can't exactly tell him I got the information from my ghostly grandmother. "When Clara and Gordy arrived, they were arguing in the hallway. I couldn't hear everything, but Clara seemed upset about something Gordy was planning. She said it wasn't right, and Gordy... well, he dismissed her concerns. Said something about how 'right' doesn't matter when there's money to be made."

Mark's eyebrows shoot up. "That's... interesting," he says slowly. "Did you hear anything else?"

I shake my head, not wanting to complicate things further with the information about June just yet. "No, that was all. I didn't think much of it at the time, but now..."

Mark nods, his expression thoughtful. "Thanks, Lena. I'll definitely look into that. But remember, we can't jump to conclusions. Everyone here had some kind of beef with Gordy, it seems."

As if to prove his point, Clara's voice suddenly rises above the murmur of the room. "This is ridiculous!" she exclaims, her earlier shock seemingly replaced by indignation. "I had nothing to do with this! If anyone had a reason to want Gordy dead, it was Pete!"

All eyes turn to Pete, who bristles visibly. "Watch what you're saying, Clara," he growls.

Clara stands, her eyes flashing. "Oh, don't act innocent, Pete. Everyone knows you've had it out for Gordy for years. Always accusing him of this or that, never able to prove anything. Must have been frustrating, wasn't it? A decorated ex-cop, unable to pin anything on the town's 'golden boy'?"

Pete takes a step forward, his fists clenching at his sides. "You don't know what you're talking about," he says, his voice low and dangerous.

Mark moves quickly, positioning himself between Pete and Clara. "Alright, that's enough," he says firmly. "We're not going to solve anything by throwing accusations around. Everyone needs to calm down and let me do my job."

As Mark works to defuse the situation, I catch Granny Ingrid's eye. She nods toward June, who is watching the scene unfold. And is that a look of satisfaction in her eyes?

I realize that if I want to get to the bottom of this, I'm going to have to do some investigating of my own. And June, with her overdone protests and defensive behavior, seems like the perfect place to start.

Taking a deep breath, I make my way over to where June is perched on the edge of an armchair, her posture rigid and her eyes darting around the room.

"June," I say softly, taking a seat next to her. "How are you holding up?"

Her head snaps towards me, her eyes narrowing slightly. "Oh, Lena, darling. What a dreadful turn of events. Who could have imagined such a thing happening at your lovely dinner party?"

I nod sympathetically, watching her face carefully. "It's horrible," I agree. "And so shocking. I mean, Gordy seemed fine all evening, didn't he? Did you notice anything... off about him?"

June's eyes flicker for just a moment before she composes herself. "Off? No, no, of course not. Gordy was... well, he was just Gordy. Loud, brash, full of himself as always."

"Mm-hmm," I murmur noncommittally. "You two seemed to have quite a lively exchange during dinner. Old friends catching up?"

June's laugh is brittle. "Friends? Hardly. Gordy and I... well, we had our differences over the years. But I certainly never wished him dead, if that's what you're implying."

I hold up my hands placatingly. "Of course not, June. I'm just trying to understand what happened. We all are."

As June launches into another round of protestations about her innocence, I listen carefully, noting every hesitation, every flicker of emotion that crosses her face.

One thing's for certain—June knows more than she's letting on. But is it guilt over Gordy's death, or something else entirely?

Chapter 7

After finishing my conversation with June, I scan the room for the next suspect. Harold catches my eye, still pacing near the window, his hands fidgeting nervously with his tie. Taking a deep breath, I make my way over to him, trying to appear casual.

"Harold," I say softly, causing him to start slightly. "How are you holding up?"

He turns to face me, his eyes wide and darting. "Lena, I-I'm fine. Just shocked, you know? Who would have thought...?" He trails off, swallowing hard.

I nod sympathetically, watching his face carefully. "I know what you mean. It's all so surreal. One minute we're having dinner, and the next..." I let the sentence hang, hoping he'll fill in the gaps.

Harold nods vigorously. "Exactly. Exactly. It's... it's terrible. Poor Gordy." He glances toward the dining room, where the paramedics have wheeled out Gordy's body. "I still can't believe it."

"Me neither," I agree. "You've known Gordy for a long time, haven't you? You must have so many memories."

Harold's expression flickers for a moment—is that guilt I see? Or just grief? "Oh, yes," he says, his voice strained. "We go way back. Had our ups and downs, of course, but that's business for you."

I raise an eyebrow. "Business? I thought you and Gordy were in different fields."

Harold's eyes widen slightly, and he quickly backpedals. "Oh, well, you know how it is in a small town. Everyone's business intersects at some point. Gordy and I... we had some joint ventures over the years. Nothing major, just... local development stuff."

I nod, filing away this information for later. "I see. And how were things between you two lately? I couldn't help but notice some tension at dinner."

Harold's hand goes back to his tie, fiddling with it nervously. "Tension? No, no, nothing like that. Just some spirited discussion. You know how Gordy could be. Always pushing buttons, stirring things up."

"Mm-hmm," I murmur noncommittally. "And that comment he made about your development project? That seemed to upset you."

Harold's face pales slightly. "Oh, that. It was nothing, really. Just Gordy being Gordy. Always hinting at things, trying to get a rise out of people. I'm sure he didn't mean anything by it."

I'm about to press further when Mark calls out, asking to speak with Harold. Harold looks almost relieved as he excuses himself, practically scurrying away from me.

As I watch him go, Granny Ingrid reappears. "That man's hiding something," she murmurs in my ear. "Did you see how he kept looking at the dining room? It's like he expected Gordy to jump out at any moment."

I nod, my mind racing. Harold's behavior is certainly suspicious, but what exactly is he hiding? And how does it connect to Gordy's death?

With the guests distracted by Mark's questioning, I decide to take the opportunity to do some investigating of my own. I make my way back to the dining room, trying to appear casual as I survey the scene of the crime.

The room is eerily quiet now, the half-eaten desserts and abandoned wine glasses a stark reminder of how quickly the evening has turned. I move slowly around the table, my eyes scanning for anything out of place.

At first, nothing seems amiss. But then, as I bend down to check under the table, something catches my eye. There, partially hidden by a chair leg, is a small glass vial.

My heart racing, I glance around to make sure no one is watching before quickly retrieving the vial. It's almost empty, but a faint residue clings to the inside. What could this have contained? And more importantly, how did it end up under the dinner table?

I'm about to pocket the vial when I hear Granny Ingrid's urgent whisper. "Lena, be careful! Harold is watching you."

I straighten up, trying to appear nonchalant as I turn toward the living room. Sure enough, Harold is sitting with Mark, but his eyes fixed on me with an intensity that sends a shiver down my spine.

Our gazes lock for a moment before he looks away, turning back to his conversation with Mark.

"Well, well," Granny Ingrid muses, her spectral form hovering beside me. "Looks like our friend Harold is more interested in this room than he's letting on. I wonder what he's so afraid we'll find?"

I nod slightly, my mind whirling with possibilities. The empty vial in my hand suddenly feels heavy with potential answers—and dangers. Whatever was in this tiny bottle, I have a sinking feeling it's the key to unraveling this whole mystery.

But as I look around at the tense faces of my guests, each hiding their own secrets and suspicions, I realize that finding the truth might be more dangerous than I'd anticipated. Because in a room full of potential killers, asking the wrong question could be deadly.

With the vial safely tucked away in my pocket, I make my way back to the living room, my mind racing with possibilities. I spot Mark standing near the fireplace where he's just finished talking to Harold. Harold has wandered off again, but Mark's brow furrowed in concentration as he jots down notes in a small notebook.

"Mark," I say softly, glancing around to ensure no one is within earshot. "Can I talk to you for a second?"

He looks up, his expression a mix of concern and curiosity. "Sure, Lena. What's up?"

I lean in close, lowering my voice. "I found something in the dining room. An empty vial, hidden under the table. I don't know if it's related to what happened, but it seems suspicious."

Mark's eyebrows shoot up, and he instinctively reaches for the badge that isn't there. He catches himself, running a hand through his hair instead. "That's... potentially significant," he says carefully. "Where is it now?"

I pat my pocket discreetly. "I've got it here. I didn't want to leave it where someone might find it or try to get rid of it."

Mark nods slowly, his expression torn. "Lena, I appreciate you telling me this, but... I'm not officially on duty tonight. I can't start collecting evidence or conducting a formal investigation without proper procedure."

I feel a flicker of frustration. "But Mark, this could be important. If that vial contained poison—"

He holds up a hand, cutting me off gently. "I know, I know. And believe me, I want to get to the bottom of this as much as you do. But we have to do this by the book. If we start handling potential evidence improperly, it could jeopardize the entire investigation."

I bite my lip, understanding his position but still feeling the urgency of the situation. "So what should we do?"

Mark sighs, glancing around the room at the tense faces of our guests. "For now, hold onto it. Don't let anyone know you have it. I'll make a call and get the official investigation started. Once the detectives arrive, we can hand it over properly."

I nod, not entirely satisfied but knowing he's right. "Okay. But Mark, there's something else going on here. These people... they're all hiding something. I can feel it."

He gives me a small, tired smile. "Welcome to law enforcement, Lena. Everyone's always hiding something. The trick is figuring out which secrets are relevant to the case at hand."

With that sobering thought, Mark excuses himself to make his call. I'm left standing by the fireplace, the weight of the vial in my pocket a constant reminder of the gravity of our situation.

Deciding to make use of the time before the official investigation begins, I make my way back to the dining room for another sweep. As I carefully examine the area around Gordy's chair, something white catches my eye, partially hidden under the tablecloth.

Glancing over my shoulder to ensure I'm alone, I crouch down and carefully pull out the object. It's a handkerchief, fine linen with delicate embroidery in one corner. As I unfold it, my heart skips a beat. There, stitched in elegant script, are the initials "P.G."

P.G.

Pete Granger?

My mind whirls with implications. What was Pete's handkerchief doing under the table, so close to where Gordy had collapsed? And why hadn't Pete mentioned losing it?

I carefully fold the handkerchief and slip it into my other pocket, opposite the vial. The plot, as they say, thickens.

As I straighten up, I feel Granny's presence nearby again. "Well, well," her ghostly voice murmurs in my ear. "Looks like our friend Pete has some explaining to do."

I nod. Pete's history with Gordy was no secret, but this... this could be the key to unraveling the whole mystery.

I make my way back to the living room, my eyes scanning for Pete's burly form. I spot him in a corner, nursing a glass of whiskey and glowering at the room at large.

As I approach, Pete's eyes narrow suspiciously. "What do you want?" he growls, his voice low and gravelly.

I paste on my most innocent smile. "Just checking in, Pete. This must be bringing back a lot of memories for you, given your history in law enforcement."

Pete grunts, taking a long swig of his drink. "Yeah, well, some things you never forget. Like the smell of death."

I suppress a shudder at his blunt words. "I can imagine. You and Gordy had quite a history too, didn't you? Must be strange, being here when..."

I trail off, watching Pete's reaction carefully. His jaw tightens, a muscle twitching in his cheek. "Gordy and I had our differences," he says gruffly. "But I didn't wish him dead, if that's what you're getting at."

"Of course not," I say quickly. "I just thought, given your background, you might have noticed something. Any details that seemed off about Gordy tonight? Before he..."

Pete's eyes bore into mine, searching for something. After a long moment, he sighs heavily. "Look, Lena. I know what you're doing. Playing detective. But take it from someone who's been there—sometimes the truth is uglier than you can imagine. You sure you want to go down this rabbit hole?"

His words send a chill down my spine, but I stand my ground. "I have to know, Pete. Gordy died in my home, at my dinner party. I can't just sit back and do nothing."

Pete nods slowly, a glimmer of respect in his eyes. "Alright then. You want to know what I noticed? Gordy was nervous tonight. Kept checking his watch, looking around like he expected someone to jump out at him. And that toast of his? That wasn't just Gordy being Gordy. He was sending a message."

I lean in, intrigued. "A message? To whom?"

Pete's eyes scan the room, lingering on each of our guests in turn. "That's the million-dollar question, isn't it? But I'll tell you this much—whoever Gordy was afraid of, they were in this room tonight. And that means they're still here."

Chapter 8

As the tension in the room continues to simmer, I spot Clara sitting alone in a corner, her face pale and her hands trembling slightly as she clutches a half-empty wine glass. Sensing an opportunity, I make my way over to her, careful to appear casual and non-threatening.

"Clara," I say softly, taking a seat next to her. "How are you holding up?"

She starts slightly at my voice, her eyes wide and haunted as they meet mine. "Oh, Lena," she says, her voice barely above a whisper. "This is all so horrible. I can't believe... I just can't believe Gordy's gone."

I nod sympathetically, watching her face carefully. "I know. It's such a shock. You and Gordy were close, weren't you? Working together for the senior center and all."

Clara's grip on her wine glass tightens. "Yes, we... we worked together quite a bit. Gordy was always so generous with his donations."

"Mm-hmm," I murmur encouragingly. "It must have been such a relief to have his support. Especially with the center's budget concerns lately."

Clara's eyes flicker to mine, a flash of suspicion quickly replaced by weariness. "Yes, well, running a non-profit is never easy. But Gordy understood the importance of our work."

I lean in slightly, keeping my voice low and sympathetic. "Clara, I couldn't help but overhear earlier... it seemed like you and Gordy were having a bit of a disagreement before dinner. Is everything okay with the center?"

Clara's face pales even further, if that's possible. She takes a long sip of her wine before responding, her voice strained. "You... you heard that? Oh, Lena, it wasn't what it sounded like. Gordy and I, we were just discussing some financial matters. Nothing serious."

I raise an eyebrow, gently pressing further. "It sounded pretty heated for a simple financial discussion. Clara, you know you can talk to me, right? If there's something going on with the center, maybe I can help."

Clara seems to deflate before my eyes, her shoulders sagging as she lets out a long, shuddering sigh. "Oh, Lena," she whispers, her voice thick with unshed tears. "It's all such a mess. I didn't want to worry anyone, but... things at the center have been difficult lately."

"Difficult how?" I prompt gently, sensing we're on the verge of a breakthrough.

Clara glances around nervously before leaning in closer. "The truth is, our funding has been... precarious. We've been relying more and more on private donations to keep our programs running. And Gordy... well, his contributions have been a lifeline."

I nod encouragingly, piecing together the puzzle. "So when I overheard you arguing..."

"It was about money," Clara admits, her voice barely audible. "Gordy, he... he was threatening to pull his donations. Said he had 'better investments' to make with his money."

The revelation hits me like a punch to the gut. "Pull his donations? But that would..."

"Ruin us," Clara finishes, a single tear escaping down her cheek. "Without Gordy's support, we'd have to cut so many programs. The meals on wheels, the daily activities, the health screenings... so many seniors in our community rely on those services. I was begging him to reconsider."

I sit back, my mind whirling with this new information. "Clara, I had no idea things were so dire. Why didn't you say something? The community would have rallied to help."

Clara shakes her head, a bitter smile twisting her lips. "Pride, I suppose. And hope. I kept thinking I could turn things around, find new donors, make it work somehow. And then Gordy made his threat, and I... I panicked."

"Is that what you were arguing about in the hallway?" I ask gently. "I heard you telling Gordy that something 'wasn't right.'"

Clara nods, her eyes distant as she recalls the conversation. "Yes. He was talking about some new development project. Said it would 'revitalize' the area, bring in more money. But the way he described it... Lena, it would have priced out most of our seniors. Turned their homes into luxury condos or something equally ridiculous."

I feel a chill run down my spine as I remember Harold's nervousness earlier, his evasiveness when I asked about his business dealings with Gordy. Could this be the connection?

"And Gordy was going to go through with this plan?" I press, trying to keep my voice neutral.

Clara nods miserably. "He said it was a 'done deal'. That I could either get on board and accept his 'generosity', or he'd pull all his funding and leave the center to fend for itself."

"Oh, Clara," I breathe, reaching out to squeeze her hand. "That must have been terrible. No wonder you were so upset at dinner."

She gives me a watery smile. "I was trying so hard to keep it together. To find a way to reason with him. I thought if I could just get him alone, make him see sense..."

Her voice trails off, and I feel a sudden chill that has nothing to do with Granny Ingrid's spectral presence. "Clara," I say carefully, "what exactly were you planning to do?"

Clara's eyes widen as she realizes the implication of my question. "No! Lena, no, I swear I didn't... I would never... Yes, I was angry with Gordy. Yes, I wanted to confront him. But I didn't kill him. You have to believe me."

As I process Clara's revelations about the senior center's financial troubles, I notice her demeanor suddenly shift. Her eyes, previously brimming with tears, now harden with a resolute glint. She leans forward, her voice dropping to a conspiratorial whisper.

"Lena," Clara says, her tone urgent, "I know I might look suspicious right now, but have you considered who really had the most reason to want Gordy dead?"

I raise an eyebrow, caught off guard by her abrupt change in tactics. "What do you mean, Clara?"

She glances around furtively before continuing, "I'm talking about Pete Granger. You know about their history, don't you? The bad blood between them goes back years."

I nod slowly, recalling the palpable tension between Pete and Gordy throughout the evening. "They did seem to have some... unresolved issues," I admit cautiously.

Clara's eyes flash with a mixture of fear and what almost looks like triumph. "Unresolved issues? That's putting it mildly. Pete's been gunning for Gordy for as long as I can remember.

Always accusing him of this or that, trying to pin some wrongdoing on him."

I lean in, intrigued despite myself. "What kind of wrongdoing?"

Clara waves her hand dismissively. "Oh, you name it. Embezzlement, fraud, even suggesting Gordy had connections to organized crime. Pete was obsessed with bringing Gordy down, but he could never prove anything."

My mind flashes to the handkerchief with Pete's initials, still hidden in my pocket. Could Clara be onto something?

"That must have been frustrating for Pete," I probe, watching Clara's reaction carefully.

She nods vigorously. "Exactly! Imagine it—a decorated ex-cop, unable to pin anything on the town's golden boy. It drove Pete mad. And tonight, well... you saw how they were at dinner. All that tension, years of resentment bubbling to the surface."

I furrow my brow, playing devil's advocate. "But Clara, couldn't the same be said about you? You admitted to arguing with Gordy, to being upset about his threats to the senior center."

Clara's face hardens, her earlier vulnerability vanishing in an instant. "That was different," she insists. "My issues with Gordy were strictly professional. Yes, I was angry about his threats to pull funding, but I would never... I could never..."

She trails off, shaking her head vehemently. "No, Lena. Whatever you might think, I didn't kill Gordy. I couldn't have. But Pete? With his grudge, his law enforcement background? He'd know how to get his hands on poison, how to administer it without being detected."

I sit back, studying Clara's face. Her arguments are persuasive, but there's something in her eyes—a flicker of desperation, perhaps?—that gives me pause.

"Clara," I say gently, "I appreciate you sharing this with me. But I have to ask—is there anything else you're not telling me? Anything at all about your relationship with Gordy that might be relevant?"

For a moment, I think I see a crack in Clara's composure, but it's gone so quickly I can't be sure I didn't imagine it.

"No, Lena," she says firmly. "I've told you everything. My relationship with Gordy was purely professional. Contentious at times, yes, but nothing more than that. Whatever happened to him tonight, I had no part in it."

I nod slowly, not entirely convinced but knowing I won't get anything more from her right now. "Alright, Clara. Thank you for being so open with me."

As I stand to leave, she catches my arm. "Lena," she says, her voice low and urgent, "be careful. There's more going on here than you know. Gordy... he had his fingers in a lot of pies, if you know what I mean. Whoever killed him, they might not stop at just one murder to keep their secrets safe."

A chill runs down my spine at her words. Before I can respond, Mark's voice cuts through the room, announcing that the official investigation team has arrived.

I give Clara a final nod before making my way back to the center of the room, my mind whirling with everything I've learned. Clara's accusations against Pete are troubling, especially given the evidence of the handkerchief. But her own evasiveness, the moments where her mask seemed to slip, leave me deeply suspicious.

As I watch the detectives file into the room, their faces grim and professional, I can't shake the feeling that we've only scratched the surface of this mystery. Clara's warning echoes in my mind—there's more going on here than I know, more secrets waiting to be uncovered.

Chapter 9

As the official investigation team begins their work, I find myself restless and eager to continue my own sleuthing. With everyone distracted by the detectives' questions, I slip away to the kitchen, intent on reexamining the scene one more time to hopefully piece things together.

The kitchen is eerily quiet, a stark contrast to the bustling hub it had been just hours earlier. I move slowly, my eyes scanning every surface for anything out of place. As I approach the pantry, a flicker of movement in the corner of my eye catches my attention. Curious, I step closer, reaching for the pantry door.

Suddenly, a strong hand shoves me from behind. I stumble forward, off-balance, into the dark confines of the pantry. Before I can react, the door slams shut behind me with a resounding thud.

"Hey!" I cry out, spinning around and grasping for the doorknob. But as I turn it, my heart sinks. The door won't budge. I'm locked in.

Panic rises in my throat as the reality of the situation sinks in. I'm trapped in a small, dark space, and the person who put me here is almost certainly Gordy's killer.

"Help!" I shout, pounding on the door with my fists. "Can anyone hear me? I'm locked in the pantry!"

My cries echo in the small space, but no response comes. Granny's Victorian house might be old, but it was built to last. I can't hear a thing through the walls, and that means it'll be almost impossible for the people in the living room to hear me—especially with all the commotion going on in there right now.

I take a deep breath, trying to calm my racing heart. "Think, Lena," I mutter to myself. "There has to be a way out of here. Granny Ingrid," I whisper desperately. "If you can hear me, I could really use some ghostly intervention right about now."

But the pantry remains silent and still. Whatever otherworldly powers Granny Ingrid possesses, apparently unlocking doors isn't one of them.

Just as I'm about to resort to shouting again, I hear footsteps approaching the kitchen. Hope surges through me.

"Hello?" I call out. "Is someone there? I'm locked in the pantry!"

The footsteps pause, then quicken. A moment later, I hear Charlie's worried voice on the other side of the door. "Lena? Is that you in there? What happened?"

Relief washes over me. "Charlie! Oh, thank goodness. Someone pushed me in here and locked the door. Can you get me out?"

"Hang on," Charlie says, her voice tense. I hear the rattle of the doorknob, followed by a frustrated grunt. "It's stuck pretty good. Let me try to find something to pry it open."

The next few minutes feel like an eternity as I listen to Charlie rummaging through drawers and muttering to herself. Finally, I hear a triumphant "Aha!" followed by the sound of metal scraping against wood.

With a loud crack, the door swings open. I stumble out, blinking in the sudden light, and find myself enveloped in Charlie's tight embrace.

"Lena!" she exclaims, her voice muffled against my shoulder. "Are you okay? I was so worried when I couldn't find you!"

I hug her back, my legs shaky with relief. "I'm fine, Charlie. Just a little shaken up. Thank you for finding me."

Charlie pulls back, her face pale and her eyes wide with concern. "What happened? How did you get locked in there?"

I shake my head, still trying to process the events myself. "I don't know. I came in here to look around, and someone shoved me from behind. I didn't see who it was."

Charlie's expression hardens. "This is serious, Lena. Someone's trying to stop you from investigating. We need to tell Mark."

As if summoned by his name, Mark appears in the kitchen doorway, his face etched with worry. "Lena? Charlie? What's going on? I've been looking everywhere for you."

Charlie quickly fills him in on finding me locked in the pantry. Mark's expression grows increasingly serious as she speaks.

"Are you okay?" he asks me, his hand resting gently on my arm. "Do you need medical attention?"

I shake my head, trying to muster a reassuring smile. "I'm fine, really. Just a bit rattled."

He nods, but his frown doesn't ease. "This is a serious escalation. Whoever did this clearly feels threatened."

A chill runs down my spine as the implications of his words sink in. "You think we're getting close to the truth?"

"It certainly seems that way," Mark says grimly. "Which means we need to be even more careful moving forward. Lena, I think it's time you shared everything you've discovered with me. No more amateur sleuthing on your own—it's too dangerous."

I nod, realizing he's right. As much as I've enjoyed playing detective, the stakes are too high now to go it alone.

"Okay," I agree. "But not here. Let's go somewhere more private."

We move to my grandfather's old study, a cozy room lined with bookshelves that's far enough from the main investigation to offer some privacy. Once the door is closed behind us, I take a deep breath and begin to recount everything I've learned.

I remind Mark about the empty vial I found under the table, careful to emphasize that I haven't touched it since putting it in my pocket. Next, I describe my conversations with the various guests—June's defensiveness, Harold's nervous behavior, Clara's revelations about the senior center's financial troubles. When I mention Pete's handkerchief, found so close to where Gordy collapsed, Mark's frown deepens.

"And you're sure the initials were P.G.?" he asks.

I nod. "Positive. It was right there, embroidered in the corner."

Mark runs a hand through his hair, his expression troubled. "That's... good evidence. But it's also circumstantial. Pete could have dropped that handkerchief at any point during the evening."

"I know," I sigh. "But combined with their history of bad blood, and Pete's law enforcement background..."

"It certainly paints a suspicious picture," Mark agrees. "But we can't rule out the others either. Harold's nervousness, Clara's financial motive, June's complex history with Gordy—they all have reasons to want him dead."

I nod, feeling the weight of the mystery pressing down on me. "So what do we do now?"

Mark is quiet for a moment, his brow furrowed in thought. Finally, he looks up, a determined glint in his eye. "I think it's time we stopped playing defense and went on the offensive. We need to gather all the guests together and confront them with what we know. We need to shake things up, see how they react when confronted with the evidence. Someone in that room killed Gordy, and it's time we flushed them out."

I nod and swallow hard. "Okay. Let's do it. But... are you sure you want me involved? You know I'm not exactly a trained investigator."

Mark's expression softens. "Lena, you've uncovered more in a few hours than most rookie detectives would in a day. Not to mention the murders you've already solved around town. You know these people, their histories, their secrets. I need you in there."

His words fill me with a warm glow of pride, tempered by the seriousness of the situation. "Okay," I agree. "When do we do this?"

"No time like the present," Mark says, standing up. "Let's gather everyone in the living room. It's time to lay all our cards on the table and see who folds under pressure."

Chapter 10

As Mark and I make our way toward the living room to gather everyone for our impromptu confrontation, Granny Ingrid materializes beside me, her expression grave and urgent.

"Lena, dear," she whispers even though I'm the only one who can hear her, "I was thinking about everything that's happened tonight, and I've just remembered something important. Something about Harold and Gordy that you need to know."

I slow my pace slightly, falling a step behind Mark to give myself a moment with Granny Ingrid. "What is it, Granny?" I murmur, keeping my voice low.

Ingrid's ghostly eyes flicker with concern as she speaks. "It was years ago, long before you were born. Harold was just starting out in business, full of ambition and big dreams. He had this deal in the works, something that would have put him on the map, made him a real player in the development world."

I nod, encouraging her to continue. Granny's spectral form shimmers as she leans in closer, her voice dropping even lower.

"But Gordy... well, Gordy had his fingers in a lot of pies even back then. He caught wind of Harold's deal and saw an opportunity. He swooped in at the last minute, used his connections and his charm, and snatched the deal right out from under Harold's nose."

My eyes widen at this revelation. "That must have devastated Harold," I whisper.

She nods solemnly. "Oh, it did more than that, dear. It nearly ruined him. Harold had put everything he had into that deal—his savings, his reputation, even mortgaged his family home. When Gordy took it all away... well, it took Harold years to recover. Some might say he never really did."

I process this information, my mind racing. It certainly puts Harold's nervous behavior throughout the night in a new light. "You think Harold never forgave Gordy for this?" I ask.

"Forgive?" Ingrid's ghostly laugh is hollow. "Oh, Lena. In all the decades I lived in this town, I've seen a lot of grudges. But the one Harold Dawson has been nursing against Gordy Jacobs? That's in a class all its own. He might play nice in public, might even do business with Gordy when he has to, but make no mistake—that wound has been festering for decades."

I bite my lip, considering the implications. Harold's increasing agitation throughout the evening, his desperate attempt to leave earlier—it all takes on a sinister new meaning in light of this old grudge.

"But Granny," I whisper, "a ruined business deal from years ago... is that really enough motive for murder?"

Ingrid's spectral form shimmers with intensity. "Lena, dear, you're thinking like a rational person. But grudges like this? They don't follow logic. They grow, they fester, they consume. And for a proud man like Harold, having to smile and play nice with the man who ruined him? Well, that's the kind of thing that can drive a person to desperate acts."

I nod slowly, the pieces starting to fall into place. But before I can respond, Ingrid's expression changes, her ghostly brow furrowing in concentration.

"There's something else," she says, her voice tinged with uncertainty. "During Gordy's toast, I noticed Harold acting... oddly."

"Oddly how?" I press, aware that we're falling further behind Mark but unable to tear myself away from this crucial information.

Ingrid's form flickers as she tries to recall the details. "He was fidgeting. More than usual, I mean. His hands were under the table, and he seemed to be fussing with something. At the time, I thought he was just nervous, but now..."

My heart races as I consider the implications. "You think he might have been doing something to Gordy's drink?"

Ingrid's ghostly shoulders lift in a shrug. "I can't be sure, dear. But given everything else... well, it certainly seems suspicious, doesn't it?"

I nod, my mind whirling with this new information. Harold's behavior throughout the night has been increasingly erratic, from his nervous glances to his attempt to leave early. And now, with the knowledge of this long-standing grudge and his suspicious actions during the toast, he's rocketed to the top of my list of suspects.

"Thank you, Granny," I whisper, my resolve strengthening. "This could be the breakthrough we needed."

Ingrid's spectral form begins to fade, but her voice lingers. "Be careful, Lena. If Harold is indeed the killer, he's already shown he's willing to go to extreme lengths to keep his secret. Watch your step, dear."

I catch Charlie's eye and subtly gesture for her to join Mark and me in the hallway. She nods, smoothly excusing herself from a conversation with Clara and making her way over to us.

Once we're huddled together, out of earshot of the other guests, I take a deep breath. "I think there are a few more things we need to discuss before we confront everyone," I whisper, glancing around to ensure we're not overheard. "About Harold, specifically."

Mark's eyebrows raise, and Charlie leans in closer, her eyes wide with curiosity. "What about him?" she asks, her voice low.

I quickly recount what Granny Ingrid told me, careful to phrase it as something I've "remembered" rather than information from a ghostly source. As I speak, I watch their faces change from curiosity to shock, then to grim understanding.

"A ruined business deal?" Charlie breathes, shaking her head. "That's... intense. No wonder Harold's been acting so squirrelly all night."

Mark nods, his brow furrowed in thought. "It certainly provides a strong motive. Grudges like that, they can eat away at a person for years. And if Gordy was still lording it over him after all this time..."

"Exactly," I agree, relieved that they're following my line of thinking. "And there's more. During Gordy's toast, Harold was acting strangely. Fidgeting with something under the table."

Charlie's eyes widen. "You think he might have been tampering with Gordy's drink?"

I shrug, trying to appear less certain than I feel. "I can't be sure, but given everything else we know, it seems suspicious, doesn't it?"

Mark nods slowly, his expression grave. "It does indeed. Harold's behavior throughout the night has been increasingly erratic. The nervous glances, the attempt to leave early... and now this information about their past. He's certainly risen to the top of our suspect list."

"So what do we do now?" Charlie asks.

I look to Mark, deferring to his law enforcement experience. He thinks for a moment before responding. "We need to confront Harold directly. Put pressure on him and see how he reacts. If he's guilty, he might crack under the strain."

"And if he's innocent?" I can't help but ask.

Mark's expression softens slightly. "Then he'll have the chance to explain himself and clear his name. Either way, we need to get to the bottom of this."

I nod, steeling myself for what's to come. "Okay. How do we do this?"

Mark outlines his plan quickly. We'll gather everyone in the living room under the guise of updating them on the investigation. Then, we'll gradually steer the conversation toward Harold and Gordy's past business dealings, watching carefully for Harold's reaction.

As we prepare to put our plan into action, I feel the excitement and trepidation coursing through me. This is it—the moment of truth. We're about to confront a potential killer, armed with nothing but circumstantial evidence and our wits.

Charlie must sense my nervousness because she reaches out and squeezes my hand. "You've got this, Lena," she whispers encouragingly. "You've always had a knack for getting to the truth. And Mark and I are right here with you."

I squeeze her hand back gratefully, drawing strength from her unwavering support. "Thanks, Charlie. I couldn't do this without you two."

Mark clears his throat, his expression serious but determined. "Ready, team? Let's do this. Remember, we're looking for any signs of guilt or nervousness from Harold. But keep an eye on the others too—we can't rule anyone out completely just yet."

With nods of agreement, we turn back toward the living room. As we enter, the quiet murmur of conversation dies away once more, all eyes turning to us expectantly.

I scan the faces of our guests, my gaze lingering on Harold. He's even paler than before, if that's possible, and I notice his hands shaking slightly as he clutches his drink.

Taking a deep breath, I step forward, ready to set our plan in motion. "Everyone, thank you for your patience," I begin, somehow keeping my voice steadier than I feel on the inside. "We have some new information that we'd like to discuss with you all."

As I speak, I watch Harold carefully. At the word "information," he flinches visibly, his eyes darting towards the exit. It's a small reaction, but in this charged atmosphere, it feels like a neon sign flashing "GUILTY."

Mark steps up beside me, his presence reassuring. "We appreciate your cooperation so far," he adds, his voice carrying the authority of his sheriff's badge, even if he's not officially on duty. "But there are still some questions we need to address. Particularly about some... past business dealings."

At this, Harold's face drains of what little color it had left. He sways slightly on his feet, and for a moment, I think he might faint.

Charlie, ever observant, seems to notice the change in his behavior, too. She subtly positions herself near Harold, looking like she's ready to catch him if he falls—or stop him if he tries to run.

But as I look at Harold's terrified face, a small doubt niggles at the back of my mind. What if we're wrong? What if this is all a terrible misunderstanding?

I push the thought aside, focusing on the task at hand. We've come too far to back down now. Whatever the truth may be, it's time to bring it to light.

With a final glance at Mark and Charlie, drawing strength from their steady presence, I take a deep breath and plunge in. "Harold," I say, my voice clear and steady, "we'd like to talk to you about your history with Gordy. Specifically, a business deal from several years ago..."

Chapter 11

I stand at the head of the dining room table, looking out at the faces of my remaining dinner guests. Mark stands to my right, his presence reassuring, while Charlie hovers near the door, ready to prevent any hasty exits. The others—June, Clara, Pete, and Harold—sit around the table, their expressions ranging from curiosity to annoyance to outright fear.

I take a moment to steel myself for what's to come. "Thank you all for joining us," I begin, my voice steadier than I feel. "As you know, we've been investigating Gordy's death, and we've uncovered some... troubling information."

June leans forward, her eyes glittering with a mixture of fear and excitement. "Well, don't keep us in suspense, dear. What have you found?"

I nod, acknowledging her impatience. "We believe we know who killed Gordy Jacobs tonight. And why."

A collective gasp ripples through the room. Clara's hand flies to her mouth, while Pete's eyes narrow suspiciously. But it's Harold's reaction I'm watching most closely. His face has gone ashen, his hands trembling as they grip the edge of the table.

"Throughout this evening," I continue, "we've all been suspects. Each of us had our reasons to be angry with Gordy, our potential motives. But as we've started digging deeper, one person's motive has stood out above the rest."

Pausing, I turn to face Harold directly. "Harold Dawson, we believe you murdered Gordy Jacobs tonight."

The room erupts into chaos. June lets out a dramatic gasp, while Clara begins to sob quietly. Pete stands abruptly, his chair scraping loudly against the floor.

But Harold... Harold just sits there, his face a mask of shock and fear.

"That's... that's ridiculous," he finally stammers, his voice weak and unconvincing. "Why would I want to kill Gordy?"

I know that what I'm about to reveal will change everything. "Because of what happened all those years ago, Harold. The business deal that Gordy stole from you. The one that nearly ruined you."

Harold's eyes widen in shock. "How... how do you know about that?"

"It doesn't matter how we know," Mark interjects smoothly. "What matters is that it provides a clear motive. A grudge you've been nursing for years."

I nod, picking up the thread. "You've never forgiven Gordy for what he did, have you, Harold? All these years, playing nice in public, doing business when you had to... but inside, that wound was still festering."

Harold shakes his head vehemently, but I can see the panic in his eyes. "No, no, you've got it all wrong. That was years ago. Water under the bridge."

"Is it?" I press. "Because your behavior tonight tells a different story. The nervous glances, the attempt to leave early... and your actions during Gordy's toast."

At this, Harold's face drains of what little color it had left. "What... what are you talking about?"

I lean forward, my voice low and intense. "You were fidgeting with something under the table during the toast, weren't you, Harold? Something small. Something like... this?"

With a flourish, I produce the empty vial I found earlier, carefully held in a handkerchief to preserve any potential evidence. Harold's eyes lock onto it, and I see the moment he realizes he's been caught.

"That's... that's not mine," he protests weakly, but the tremor in his voice betrays him.

"We found it under the table," I explain, "right near where you were sitting. And given your history with Gordy, your behavior tonight..."

Harold's composure finally cracks. He slumps in his chair, his head in his hands. "You don't understand," he says, his voice muffled. "You can't possibly understand what he did to me."

The room falls silent, all eyes on Harold as he looks up, his face a mask of pain and anger. "That deal... it wasn't just business. It was everything. My future, my family's future. I'd put everything on the line, and Gordy... he swept in and took it all away like it was nothing."

Tears begin to stream down Harold's face as he continues. "Do you know what it's like, living in this town all these years? Watching him strut around, flaunting his success? Success that should have been mine?"

I feel a pang of sympathy, despite everything. "But Harold, that was years ago. Why now? Why tonight?"

Harold lets out a bitter laugh. "Why tonight? Because he was going to do it again. That development project he mentioned... it was mine. I'd been working on it for months, lining up investors, securing permits. And then I found out

Gordy had wormed his way in, was going to push me out. Again."

The pieces fall into place, and I nod slowly. "So when he made that toast, hinting at his plans..."

"I just... snapped," Harold finishes, his voice barely above a whisper. "I couldn't let him ruin me again. I couldn't."

"Harold," I say gently, "we know how you did it. During Gordy's toast, when everyone's attention was on him, you used that moment to poison his drink."

Harold's eyes widen, but he doesn't interrupt. I continue, my voice steady despite the gravity of the accusation. "The vial we found under the table contained the poison, didn't it? You must have dropped it in your haste to dispose of the evidence."

The room is deathly silent as everyone processes this information. Clara lets out a small gasp, while June's hand flies to her mouth in shock. Pete's expression is grim, his years of police experience clearly allowing him to see the logic in my deduction.

Harold remains silent for a long moment, his shoulders slumped in defeat. When he finally speaks, his voice is barely above a whisper. "I... I didn't mean for it to happen like this. I just wanted him to stop. To feel, for once, what it was like to lose everything."

The confession hangs in the air, heavy with the weight of years of resentment and a moment of fatal decision. I feel a complex mix of emotions—satisfaction at solving the mystery, sadness for the lives ruined, and a deep, unsettling understanding of how past hurts can fester and grow into something monstrous.

"Harold Dawson," Mark says, "you're under arrest for the murder of Gordy Jacobs."

As Mark begins to read Harold his rights, the room remains in stunned silence. The other guests watch in horror and fascination as Harold is handcuffed, the reality of the situation finally sinking in.

I catch Charlie's eye across the room. She gives me a small, sad smile—a recognition of a mystery solved, but at a terrible cost. I nod back, feeling the weight of the evening settle on my shoulders.

As Harold is led away, I can't help but reflect on the chain of events that led us here. A dinner party meant to raise funds for the senior center has instead exposed the dark underbelly of our small town—the grudges, the secrets, the simmering resentments that can, in a moment of weakness, lead to tragedy.

The sound of sirens grows louder in the distance, signaling the arrival of Mark's deputies. I sink into a nearby chair, suddenly exhausted. We've uncovered the truth, brought a killer to justice. But as I look around at the shocked and tearful faces of my guests, I can't help but feel that this is just the beginning.

Because in our small town, secrets have a way of rippling outward, touching everyone in their path. The revelations of tonight will have consequences that none of us can yet foresee. Relationships will be strained, trust will be broken, and the comfortable illusion of small-town tranquility has been shattered.

As the first police officers enter the room, I close my eyes and take a deep breath. The mystery may be solved, but I have a feeling our troubles are far from over. The emotional aftermath of this evening will linger long after the police tape comes down and the gossip dies away.

The night is drawing to a close, and I find myself standing at the window, looking out at the quiet streets of our town. Tomorrow, the news will spread. Tomorrow, we'll all have to face the reality of what happened here tonight.

But for now, in this moment of quiet after the storm, I allow myself a small sense of pride. Because tonight, a reluctant hostess turned amateur sleuth solved a murder and brought a killer to justice.

Again.

Chapter 12

As the shock of the evening's events starts to wear off, my remaining guests begin to stir, preparing to leave. The atmosphere is heavy with a mix of emotions—relief that the truth has been uncovered, sadness for the loss of Gordy, and a lingering tension as everyone processes their role in the night's drama.

I stand by the front door, saying goodbye to each guest as they depart. Clara leaves first, her eyes red-rimmed from crying, mumbling something about needing to inform the senior center board. Pete follows shortly after, his gruff exterior softened slightly as he gives me a nod of grudging respect.

As I watch them go, I feel a presence at my elbow. Turning, I find June standing there, her usual haughty demeanor replaced by an uncharacteristic vulnerability.

"Lena, dear," she says softly, her voice lacking its usual sharp edge. "Might I have a word with you in private before I go?"

Surprised by her request, I nod, leading her to a quiet corner of the living room. June glances around, ensuring we're out of earshot of the lingering police officers and other guests.

"I... I wanted to thank you," she begins, her voice barely above a whisper. "For not letting Gordy's death go unsolved. For uncovering the truth."

I blink in surprise, not expecting this from June of all people. "Of course," I reply, unsure of what else to say.

Her eyes, usually so sharp and calculating, are now filled with only grief and gratitude in equal parts. "You must understand," she continues, "Gordy and I... our relationship was complicated. We had our differences, our arguments. But there was a time, a long time ago, when things were different."

She pauses, lost in memory for a moment. "We were young, full of dreams and ambition. Gordy had this charm about him, this way of making you feel like anything was possible. Of course, that same charm could be infuriating when turned against you."

I nod, beginning to understand the complex history between June and Gordy. "It sounds like you cared for him deeply," I say gently.

June's laugh is soft and tinged with sadness. "Oh, I did. More than I care to admit, even now. But life has a way of complicating things, doesn't it? Gordy's ambition, my pride... we both said and did things we couldn't take back."

She takes a deep breath, composing herself. "What I'm trying to say, Lena, is that despite our public animosity, I never wished Gordy dead. The thought of him being murdered, of his killer going free... it was unbearable."

I reach out, squeezing June's hand gently. "I understand. And I'm glad I could help bring some closure, for everyone's sake."

June nods, a small smile tugging at the corners of her mouth. "You did more than that, dear. You showed real courage tonight, real determination. It reminds me of your grandmother, you know. Ingrid always had a knack for getting to the heart of matters, seeing what others missed."

At the mention of Granny Ingrid, I feel a familiar presence nearby. Out of the corner of my eye, I catch a glimpse of her spectral form, nodding approvingly at June's words.

"Thank you, June," I say, feeling a warmth spread through me at the comparison to my grandmother. "That means a lot to me."

June straightens up, some of her usual poise returning. "Yes, well, don't let it go to your head," she says, but there's a newfound warmth in her tone. "This town needs someone like you, Lena. Someone who's not afraid to dig beneath the surface, to uncover the truth no matter how uncomfortable it might be."

With that, she gives my hand a final squeeze before turning to leave. As she reaches the door, she pauses, looking back at me. "And Lena? Don't be a stranger. My door is always open if you need... well, if you need anything."

I nod, watching as June disappears into the night. As I close the door behind her, I can't help but feel that something has shifted. Not just with June, but with the entire town. The events of tonight have peeled back a layer, exposing the complex web of relationships and histories that bind us all together.

Lost in thought, I nearly jump when I feel a hand on my shoulder. Turning, I find Mark standing there, his expression a mixture of exhaustion and something softer, more vulnerable.

"Quite a night, huh?" he says, a wry smile tugging at his lips.

I let out a small laugh, the absurdity of the understatement hitting me. "You could say that again. Not exactly the quiet, sophisticated dinner party I'd planned."

Mark's smile widens, and I feel a flutter in my stomach. "About that," he says, his voice taking on a hesitant tone. "I know this evening didn't go quite as we expected, but... I was wondering if you'd like to try again sometime? Under less dramatic circumstances, of course. Maybe just the two of us next time?"

I feel a blush creeping up my cheeks, a warmth spreading through me that has nothing to do with the lingering adrenaline of the night's events. "They say the third time's a charm..."

Mark's eyes light up, and for a moment, the weight of the evening seems to lift from his shoulders. "Great," he says, sounding almost boyishly excited. "How about next Friday? I know a little place just outside of town. No murder mysteries, I promise. Just good food and good company."

I laugh, feeling lighter than I have all night. "Sounds perfect. Although, I have to warn you - life around here is never uneventful. Not with me around, apparently."

Mark's smile turns tender as he reaches out, tucking a stray strand of hair behind my ear. "I wouldn't have it any other way," his deep voice rumbles.

As we stand there, the promise of another future date hanging between us, I feel Granny Ingrid's presence once more. Her spectral form materializes near the staircase, a knowing smile on her face.

"Well done, Lena dear," she says, her voice carrying that otherworldly echo. "You've not only solved a mystery but opened your heart to new possibilities. Remember, life is full of surprises—some tragic, some wonderful. It's how we face them that defines us."

I give her a small nod, careful not to alert Mark to her presence. As Granny Ingrid fades away, I turn back to Mark, feeling a surge of excitement for what the future might hold.

"So," I say, a playful smile tugging at my lips. "Next Friday. It's a date."

Mark's answering grin is enough to make my heart skip a beat. "It's a date," he confirms.

As we stand there, the last remnants of the chaotic evening fading away, I can't help but feel a sense of anticipation. Yes, life in New Oslo will never be truly quiet—not with Granny

Ingrid's ghostly presence, not with the secrets and histories that lurk beneath the surface of our small town. But with Mark by my side and my newfound talent for uncovering the truth, I'm ready to face whatever mysteries come our way.

And as I catch one last glimpse of Granny Ingrid's approving smile before she vanishes completely, I know that whatever comes next, I'll face it with courage, curiosity, and an open heart. Because in New Oslo, you never know when a simple dinner party might turn into the adventure of a lifetime.

Chapter 13

Friday evening arrives with a flutter of anticipation in my stomach. I stand before my bedroom mirror, scrutinizing my reflection for the umpteenth time. The navy blue dress I've chosen feels both comfortable and elegant, but doubt creeps in as I smooth nonexistent wrinkles.

"Oh, for heaven's sake, Lena," Granny Ingrid's spectral voice chimes in, making me jump. "You look lovely. Stop fussing!"

I turn to see her ghostly form perched on the edge of my bed, a mischievous twinkle in her eye. "Granny! You startled me."

She waves a translucent hand dismissively. "Occupational hazard of being a ghost, dear. Now, are you ready for your big date with the dashing Sheriff Mark?"

I feel a blush creeping up my cheeks. "As ready as I'll ever be, I suppose. It's just... it's been a while since I've been on a proper date. You remember the first time he and I tried to go out to the Bake-Off. And then after everything that happened at the dinner party..."

Granny Ingrid's laugh tinkles like wind chimes. "Ah, yes. Nothing like a murder investigation to spice up a budding romance!"

"Granny!" I exclaim, but I can't help chuckling. "It's not funny. What if things are weird between us now?"

She floats over to me, her spectral form shimmering in the light. "Lena, dear, that man has seen you at your most determined and clever. If anything, recent events have only made him more smitten."

I smile, grateful for her reassurance. "You think so?"

"I know so," she says with a wink. "Now, let me impart some wisdom about modern dating."

I raise an eyebrow, amused. "Granny, you've been... well, you know. And Grandpa has been deceased for over a decade. What do you know about modern dating?"

She puts her hands on her hips, looking indignant. "I'll have you know I've been keeping up with the times! These walls aren't as thick as you might think, and your cousin Meredith is quite the chatterbox when she visits."

I can't help but laugh at the image of my ghostly grandmother eavesdropping on my cousin's gossip sessions. "Okay then, dating guru Granny. What's your advice?"

She straightens up, adopting a mock-serious tone. "First, remember the sacred rule of modern courtship: thou shalt not check thy phone every two minutes."

I roll my eyes, but she continues undeterred. "Second, if he suggests 'Netflix and chill,' be aware that it's not as innocent as it sounds."

"Granny!" I gasp, feeling my face flame red.

She cackles, clearly enjoying my discomfort. "What? I may be dead, but I'm not oblivious!"

Shaking my head, I turn back to the mirror for one last check. "Any actual advice?"

Her expression softens as she meets my gaze in the reflection. "Just be yourself, Lena. That's who Mark has fallen for, after all. The clever, kind, slightly nosy woman who isn't afraid to stand up for what's right."

I feel a lump form in my throat at her words. "Thank you, Granny."

The doorbell rings, making me jump. Granny Ingrid gives me an encouraging smile. "Go get him, tiger!"

As I hurry downstairs, I hear her call out, "And remember, if he turns out to be a secret serial killer, you know who to call!"

Laughing despite my nerves, I reach for the door handle and open the door to find Mark standing on my porch, looking handsome in a blue button-down shirt and dark jeans. He's holding a small bouquet of wildflowers, and the sight makes my heart skip a beat.

"Hi," I say, suddenly feeling shy.

"Hi," he replies, a warm smile spreading across his face. "You look beautiful, Lena."

I feel a blush creeping up my cheeks. "Thank you. You clean up pretty well yourself, Sheriff."

He chuckles, then holds out the flowers. "These are for you. I, uh, picked them myself. I hope that's okay."

"You picked them?" I ask, taking the bouquet and inhaling their sweet scent. "Should I be concerned about any angry gardeners coming after us tonight?"

Mark's eyes widen in mock horror. "Oh no, you've discovered my secret criminal past. I'm a notorious flower thief."

I laugh, feeling some of the tension dissipate. "Well, as long as you're not a murderer, I think we're okay."

As soon as the words leave my mouth, I cringe. "Oh God, I'm sorry. That was probably in poor taste, given... everything."

But Mark just shakes his head, still smiling. "It's okay, Lena. If we can't joke about it, how else are we supposed to deal with the fact that our second almost-date turned into a murder investigation?"

I relax, grateful for his understanding. "True. Although I hope this one doesn't follow the same pattern. I'm determined to leave my detective hat at home tonight."

"Darn," Mark says, snapping his fingers in mock disappointment. "And here I was, hoping we could solve the mystery of the missing dessert menu."

I snicker, then realize we're still standing in the doorway. "Oh! Come in for a second while I put these in water?"

As Mark steps inside, I hear a faint whisper that sounds suspiciously like Granny Ingrid saying, "Nice flowers. Better not be from my yard!"

I shoot a glare in the direction of the voice, hoping Mark didn't hear anything. Luckily, he seems preoccupied with looking around the entryway.

"You know," he says thoughtfully, "As crazy as it sounds, I don't think I've ever really taken the time to look around in here before. It's really nice. Especially when I'm not distracted by a murder case."

"Thanks," I reply, coming back from the kitchen with the flowers now in a vase. "It's been in my family for generations. Sometimes I think the walls have soaked up all the stories over the years."

If only he knew how true that was, given Granny Ingrid's continued presence.

"I can imagine," Mark says, his eyes twinkling. "Any ghost stories?"

I nearly choke, covering it with a cough. "Oh, you know, the usual creaky floorboards and strange noises. Nothing too exciting."

From the corner of my eye, I see Granny Ingrid appear, looking indignant. "Nothing too exciting? I'll have you know I'm a very exciting ghost!"

Ignoring her, I turn to Mark. "Shall we get going? I'm excited to see this place you mentioned."

He nods, offering me his arm in a gallant gesture. "Your chariot awaits, my lady."

As we walk to his car, I can't help but feel a mixture of excitement and nervousness. This is Mark, I remind myself. The same Mark I've known since high school. Just because we're going on a date doesn't mean things have to be weird.

But as he opens the car door for me, his hand brushing mine, I feel a spark of electricity that's definitely new. New-ish, anyway. Maybe, I think as I settle into the seat, a little bit of weirdness isn't such a bad thing after all.

As Mark pulls away from my house, I can't help but sneak glances at him. In the soft glow of the dashboard lights, his profile looks particularly handsome. He catches me looking and grins.

"See something you like?" he teases.

I feel my cheeks heat up but decide to play along. "Oh, you know, just admiring the view. It's not often I get to see the sheriff out of uniform."

Mark chuckles. "Well, I figured you've gotten accustomed to seeing my badge and gun on our dates by now. Although given your penchant for stumbling into mysteries, maybe I should have brought them just in case."

I laugh, feeling some of the tension ease. "Hey, I'll have you know I can go at least a week without encountering any dead bodies or nefarious plots."

"A whole week?" Mark gasps in mock astonishment. "I'm impressed. That must be some kind of record for you."

I swat his arm playfully. "Oh, hush. I'm not that bad."

He grins, taking one hand off the wheel to catch mine. "I'm just teasing. Although I have to admit, your knack for solving mysteries is pretty impressive. Not to mention attractive."

I feel a flutter in my stomach at his words and the warmth of his hand on mine. "Careful, Sheriff. Keep talking like that, and I might think you're only interested in me for my detective skills."

Mark's expression softens as he glances at me. "Trust me, Lena. Your brilliant mind is just one of the many things I find irresistible about you."

The sincerity in his voice makes my heart skip a beat. To lighten the suddenly intense mood, I quip, "Flattery will get you everywhere, you know."

He laughs, giving my hand a squeeze before returning his to the wheel. "I'll keep that in mind. So, tell me something I don't know about you, Lena Larsen."

I ponder for a moment. "Hmm... Oh! Did you know I once won a pie-eating contest at the county fair?"

Mark's eyebrows shoot up. "You? Miss prim and proper Lena Larsen, face-deep in pie?"

I grin, remembering the day. "Hey, don't let the fancy dresses fool you. I've got a competitive streak a mile wide. Plus, it was cherry pie. My absolute favorite."

"I'm learning all sorts of interesting things about you tonight," Mark says, shaking his head in amusement. "Any other hidden talents I should know about?"

"Well," I say, tapping my chin thoughtfully, "I can touch my nose with my tongue. Want to see?"

Mark bursts out laughing. "Maybe later. I'd hate for you to strain yourself before dinner."

As we drive, the conversation flows easily, touching on lighter topics like our favorite movies (he's a sucker for old westerns, while I prefer classic mysteries), our first jobs (he mowed lawns, I babysat), and our most embarrassing moments in high school (his involved an unfortunate incident with the school mascot costume, mine a spectacular fall during a pep rally).

Before I know it, we're pulling up to a charming little bistro nestled at the edge of a picturesque lake. The setting sun casts a golden glow over the water, and fairy lights twinkle in the trees surrounding the restaurant.

"Oh, Mark," I breathe, taking in the romantic scene. "This is beautiful."

He smiles, looking pleased with my reaction. "I'm glad you like it. I discovered this place a few months ago and have been waiting for the right moment to share it with someone special."

The warmth in his eyes as he says this makes my heart flutter. As he comes around to open my door, I'm struck by how natural this feels—being here with Mark, on a real date. All the nervousness from earlier seems to have melted away, replaced by a sense of rightness.

As we walk towards the entrance, Mark's hand finds the small of my back, guiding me gently. The touch sends a pleasant shiver up my spine.

"Ready for a mystery-free evening?" he asks, his eyes twinkling with mischief.

I laugh, leaning into him slightly. "Absolutely. Although with my luck, we'll probably uncover a secret smuggling ring operating out of the kitchen."

Mark grins, holding the door open for me. "Well, if we do, at least I'm in good company. Now, shall we see what non-criminal delights await us inside?"

With a nod and a smile, I step into the warmth of the bistro and find that the interior is just as charming as its exterior. Soft jazz plays in the background, and the warm glow of candles on each table creates an intimate atmosphere. A smiling hostess leads us to a cozy corner table with a view of the lake.

As we settle into our seats, I can't help but feel a flutter of nerves return. This is really happening—I'm on a date with Mark. The Mark I've known for years, but suddenly see in a completely new light since moving back to New Oslo a few months ago.

"So," Mark says, picking up his menu with a grin, "what do you think the chances are of finding a coded message hidden in these entree descriptions?"

I laugh, grateful for his attempt to break the ice. "Pretty slim, I'd say. Although that 'Chef's Mystery Special' does sound intriguing."

"Ooh, risky," Mark says, raising an eyebrow. "Are you brave enough to order something when you don't know what it is?"

I pretend to consider it seriously. "Well, given my recent track record with surprises, maybe I should play it safe tonight."

Our waiter arrives, introducing himself as Tony and rattling off the evening's specials. As he describes a particularly mouthwatering risotto, I notice Mark watching me with a soft smile.

"What?" I ask, feeling self-conscious.

He shakes his head, still smiling. "Nothing. It's just... it's nice to see you like this. Relaxed, you know? Not trying to solve any crimes or uncover any dark secrets."

I feel a warmth spread through me at his words. "It is nice, isn't it? Although I have to admit, part of me is waiting for the other shoe to drop. For Tony to suddenly reveal he's an undercover agent or something."

Mark chuckles. "Well, if he is, he's very committed to his cover. Did you see how enthusiastically he described that creme brulee?"

We place our orders—the risotto for me, a steak for Mark—and settle into comfortable conversation. As we wait for our food, I find myself marveling at how easy this feels. There's a new energy between us now, a spark that makes every glance and smile feel charged with possibility.

"So, Sheriff," I say, taking a sip of my wine, "tell me something about yourself that I don't already know."

Mark leans back, considering. "Hmm... Okay, here's one. When I was a kid, I wanted to be a magician."

I nearly choke on my wine. "A magician? You?"

He nods, grinning sheepishly. "Had the whole kit—top hat, wand, deck of trick cards. I was convinced I was going to be the next David Copperfield."

The image of a young Mark in a magician's outfit is too adorable for words. "What happened to that dream?"

"Reality," he says with a dramatic sigh. "Turns out, I'm terrible at sleight of hand. Nearly set my mom's curtains on fire trying to do a 'magical flame' trick. After that, she gently suggested I might want to consider other career options."

I'm laughing so hard I have to put down my wine glass. "Oh, I would have paid good money to see that!"

"Yeah, yeah, laugh it up," Mark says, but he's smiling too. "What about you? Any childhood dreams that didn't quite pan out?"

I think for a moment. "Well, there was a brief period where I was convinced I was going to be a famous opera singer."

Now it's Mark's turn to look surprised. "Opera? You?"

"Hey, don't look so shocked," I say, pretending to be offended. "I'll have you know I have a lovely singing voice."

"Oh, I don't doubt it," Mark says quickly. "It's just... opera seems so..."

"Dramatic?" I supply. "Over-the-top? Not very Lena-like?"

He nods, looking relieved that I'm not actually upset.

"Well, that was kind of the appeal," I explain. "I was always the quiet, bookish kid. Opera seemed like this whole other world where it was okay to be loud and passionate and larger than life."

Mark's expression softens. "I can see that. So what happened?"

I shrug. "Reality, just like with your magic career. Turns out, while I can carry a tune, I'm not exactly Maria Callas."

"Lucky for me," Mark says, reaching across the table to take my hand. "I much prefer my crime-solving partner to an opera diva."

The warmth of his hand on mine sends a pleasant tingle up my arm. Before I can respond, Tony arrives with our food, breaking the moment.

As we dig into our meals, which are every bit as delicious as promised, the conversation continues to flow easily. We swap stories about some of his most memorable cases, our favorite spots in town, our families. With each passing minute, I feel myself falling a little bit more for this man who can make me laugh, challenge my mind, and make me feel completely at ease all at once.

By the time we're splitting a slice of that much-praised creme brulee, I'm certain of two things: one, this is the best date I've ever been on, and two, I'm in serious danger of falling head over heels for the man sitting across from me.

As we savor the last bites of our dessert, Mark glances at his watch and then gives me a mysterious smile. "You know, the night's still young. How do you feel about a little adventure?"

I raise an eyebrow, intrigued. "Adventure? Should I be worried?"

He chuckles, shaking his head. "No dead bodies or criminal masterminds involved, I promise. Just a little surprise I think you might enjoy."

"Well, now I'm definitely curious," I say, feeling a flutter of excitement. "Lead the way, Sheriff."

Mark pays the bill despite my protests to split it, and we head out into the cool evening air. As we walk back to his car, he takes my hand, intertwining our fingers. The simple gesture feels so natural, so right, that it takes my breath away for a moment.

We drive for about ten minutes, the road winding up into the hills surrounding New Oslo. As we climb higher, the lights of the town spread out below us like a glittering carpet.

Finally, Mark pulls off onto a small gravel path, parking in a clearing that overlooks the entire valley. The view is breathtaking—the town's lights twinkling below, the surrounding countryside bathed in moonlight, and above, a canopy of stars more brilliant than I've ever seen.

"Oh, Mark," I breathe, stepping out of the car. "This is incredible."

He comes around to my side, wrapping an arm around my waist. "I thought you might like it. It's my favorite spot to come and clear my head."

We stand there for a moment, taking in the view. Then Mark leads me to a small bench positioned perfectly to overlook the valley.

As we sit, a comfortable silence falls between us. I lean into Mark's side, and he tightens his arm around me.

"You know," I say softly, "when I was planning that charity dinner, I never imagined it would lead to... well, all of this."

Mark chuckles, the sound rumbling through his chest. "You mean you didn't plan on a murder investigation as a charity event? I'm shocked."

I playfully swat his arm. "Very funny. But seriously, Mark... I'm glad it happened. Not the murder part, obviously, but... this. Us."

He turns to look at me, his eyes soft in the moonlight. "Me too. Really glad."

For a moment, we just look at each other, the air between us charged with possibility. Then, slowly, Mark leans in. I close my eyes as his lips meet mine in a soft, sweet kiss.

When we part, I can't help but smile. "Well, Sheriff, I'd say that was worth the wait."

He grins, pulling me closer. "Glad to hear it, Ms. Larsen. Though I think we might need a bit more practice, just to be sure."

Laughing, I lean in for another kiss, marveling at how right this feels. As we sit there, trading kisses and quiet conversation under the stars, I feel a sense of contentment wash over me.

All too soon, it's time to head back. As we drive toward my house, Mark reaches over to take my hand, and I marvel at how natural the gesture already feels.

"So," he says, a hint of nervousness in his voice, "on a scale of one to ten, how would you rate this evening? Keeping in mind, of course, that we managed to avoid any murders or international conspiracies."

I pretend to consider seriously. "Well, let's see. Delicious food, beautiful scenery, charming company... I'd say it's at least a nine."

"Only a nine?" Mark asks, feigning disappointment. "What would it take to bump it up to a perfect ten?"

I grin mischievously. "Well, I suppose that depends on how the good-night kiss goes."

Mark's answering smile sends a flutter through my stomach. "I'll do my best not to disappoint, then."

As we pull up in front of my house, I feel a mix of contentment and reluctance for the evening to end. Mark comes around to open my door—ever the gentleman—and walks me to my front porch.

We stand there for a moment, both seemingly reluctant to say goodnight. Finally, Mark breaks the silence.

"Lena," he says softly, taking both my hands in his, "I had a wonderful time tonight."

I smile up at him. "So did I, Mark. It was perfect."

He raises an eyebrow. "Perfect? I thought we were still at a nine."

Laughing, I step closer to him. "Well, there's still one more thing to factor in, isn't there?"

Mark's eyes darken slightly as he pulls me closer. "I suppose there is."

As his lips meet mine, I feel like I'm melting. This kiss is different from our earlier ones—deeper, more passionate, full of promise for what's to come. When we finally part, we're both a little breathless.

"So," Mark murmurs, his forehead resting against mine, "did we make it to a ten?"

I pretend to think about it for a moment. "Hmm... I'd say it's at least an eleven."

He grins, looking pleased with himself. "High praise indeed. Though I think we might need a few more dates to really perfect our technique."

"A few more dates, huh?" I say, trying to sound casual despite the excitement bubbling up inside me. "Did you have anything specific in mind?"

Mark's smile softens. "Well, there's a new exhibit opening at the art museum in a couple of weeks. I thought maybe we could check it out together. Unless, of course, you're worried about uncovering an art forgery ring or something."

I laugh, shaking my head. "I think I can manage to behave myself for one afternoon. It's a date."

As Mark leans in for one last kiss, I hear a faint, familiar voice on the wind. "About time, you two!"

I stiffen slightly, recognizing Granny Ingrid's ghostly interference. Mark pulls back, looking concerned.

"Everything okay?" he asks.

I nod quickly, shooting a glare towards the general direction of Granny's voice. "Everything's perfect. Just... thought I heard something."

Mark looks around, then shrugs. "Must be the wind. Or maybe your house really is haunted after all."

If only he knew how right he was. But that's a mystery for another day.

"Goodnight, Lena," Mark says softly, giving my hand one last squeeze before stepping back.

"Goodnight, Mark," I reply, already looking forward to our next date.

As I watch him drive away, I can't help but smile. Who would have thought that a charity dinner gone wrong would lead to this? But then again, in New Oslo, you never know where the next adventure—or the next romance—might be waiting.

Also by Sloane Finley

Death by Dessert Series

Death by Chocolate Cupcake[1]

Death by Devil's Food Cake[2]

Ghostly Gumshoe Series

Granny's Ghost and the Haunted Homicide[3]

Granny's Ghost and the Poisoned Punch[4]

---

1. https://www.amazon.com/Death-Chocolate-Cupcake-Dessert-Mystery-ebook/dp/B0DPGS8S8Z
2. https://www.amazon.com/gp/product/B0DR7GTS38
3. https://www.amazon.com/gp/product/B0DFZR8LV6
4. https://www.amazon.com/gp/product/B0DGNN9QNK

Granny's Ghost and the Bake-Off Bribe[5]
Granny's Ghost and the Deadly Dinner Party[6]
Granny's Ghost and the Movie Night Murder[7]
Granny's Ghost and the Murdered Medium[8]
Granny's Ghost and the Basement Burial[9]
Granny's Ghost and the Murdered Magician[10]
Granny's Ghost and the Deadly Delphinium[11]
Granny's Ghost and the Killer Caroler[12]
Granny's Ghost and the Fatal Fashion Show[13]
Granny's Ghost and the Cook-Off Killer[14]
Ghostly Gumshoe Collection (Books 1 - 3)[15]

Fur-ensic Files Series
Fetch Me a Felon[16]
Best in Show, Worst in Murder[17]

---

5. https://www.amazon.com/gp/product/B0DHB1CBQL
6. https://www.amazon.com/gp/product/B0DJ7PW47X
7. https://www.amazon.com/gp/product/B0DJQ4R3L1
8. https://www.amazon.com/gp/product/B0DKB6Y47K
9. https://www.amazon.com/gp/product/B0DL3GRP97
10. https://www.amazon.com/gp/product/B0DLVJJJ33
11. https://www.amazon.com/gp/product/B0DMYJ5RQ6
12. https://www.amazon.com/gp/product/B0DNY9H8YM
13. https://www.amazon.com/gp/product/B0DQHXXW7Z
14. https://www.amazon.com/gp/product/B0DRWFBDK4
15. https://www.amazon.com/Ghostly-Gumshoe-Collection-Paranormal-Mystery-ebook/dp/B0DHPDBYQ9
16. https://www.amazon.com/gp/product/B0DFVQMWV5
17. https://www.amazon.com/gp/product/B0DHPWBRFT

Dachshund Dynasty[18]

Fur-ensic Files Complete Collection (Books 1 - 3)[19]

18. https://www.amazon.com/gp/product/B0DJG9KWYL
19. https://www.amazon.com/Fur-ensic-Files-Collection-Sloane-Finley-ebook/dp/B0DJZV9ZLZ

www.ingramcontent.com/pod-product-compliance
Ingram Content Group UK Ltd.
Pitfield, Milton Keynes, MK11 3LW, UK
UKHW021013180825
7441UKWH00015B/72

9 798231 957750